Praise for Nicole Kimberling's
Ghost Star Night

"I personally find Ghost Star Night a far superior fantasy story... If you are looking for an interesting and entertaining steampunk fantasy with some romance, this one may fit the bill."

~ *Mrs. Giggles, MrsGiggles.com*

"The fantasy world created by Nicole Kimberling is a lush, colorful mix taken from different areas of fantasy, all blended together to create a unique world...I found Ghost Star Night to be a fascinating read...I was engrossed from start to finish and applaud the author for creating such a distinctive setting for her novel."

~ *Jenre, Reviews by Jessewave*

"It's a stunningly good piece of speculative fiction writing-- truly one of the best I've read in a very long time."

~ *Ann Somerville, Uniquely Pleasurable*

Look for these titles by
Nicole Kimberling

Now Available:

Happy Snak

Ghost Star Night

Nicole Kimberling

A SAMHAIN PUBLISHING, LTD. publication.

Samhain Publishing, Ltd.
577 Mulberry Street, Suite 1520
Macon, GA 31201
www.samhainpublishing.com

Ghost Star Night
Copyright © 2010 by Nicole Kimberling
Print ISBN: 978-1-60504-736-2
Digital ISBN: 978-1-60504-638-9

Editing by Anne Scott
Cover by Anne Cain

First Samhain Publishing, Ltd. electronic publication: August 2009
First Samhain Publishing, Ltd. print publication: June 2010

Chapter One

Adam loved the music. And the red and amber lights flashing up from the luminous floor. And the crush of dancing bodies. And the strong, sophisticated cocktails. In short, he loved this club.

Pulsing electronic beats throbbed through the smoky air so loud and so low that he felt it deep in his chest. The scenery wasn't bad either. Although the club was mixed, both gay and straight, noble and common, the dark-haired man eyeing him from the neon-lit bar had to be a courtier. Not from Adam's own West Court, but maybe from the North Court. He had that academic look that men from the North Court had. Adam smiled, his signature move. Normally, smiling could not be called a signature move, but Adam fully understood the power of his full lips and straight, white teeth. Smiling elevated him from good-looking blond to sexy hunk.

The lord from North Court, sitting at the bar, sat up straight and motioned Adam closer.

From deep within his pocket, Adam's phone vibrated. He decided to ignore it, then it pulsed again, in that special rhythm. Lady Langdon, his godmother, needed him. With regret he shook his head at Lord North Court and bounded up the staircase that led to street level. He rushed up to the big gorilla doorman who controlled the line of well-dressed hopefuls waiting to get inside. The gorilla bared his teeth and his black fur bristled as Adam jostled past him and out into the humid summer night.

"How may I serve you, my lady?" he answered, slightly out of breath.

"You need to get Drake now!" Lady Langdon shouted so loudly that Adam had to pull the phone from his ear.

"Drake?" Adam squinted down the dark street, feeling too dazed with nightlife to immediately understand what she wanted from him at this hour. "The magician of the Black Tower?"

"Is there another?" Lady Langdon snapped. "Go and bring him! Promise him whatever is necessary, with the exception of your soul. You'll need that later."

"I would think that mere cash would be enough to encourage him." As far as Adam knew, Drake was among the last of the freelancers. A gun for hire in a city where almost every other magician was allied to one of the four courts.

"That's why thinking is not one of the attributes for which you are best known," Lady Langdon said. "Don't fail me."

Adam rounded the corner and found his car and driver waiting. His driver, an elderly orangutan called Karl, had been lightly dozing in the front seat, and started awake when Adam rapped on the hood. He straightened his hat and scrambled out to open the door for Adam, who tumbled into the car's backseat with the lax grace of the practically unconscious. He waited for his driver to resettle himself behind the wheel and said, "To the Black Tower."

Karl nodded and signed, "Did you have a good night, boss?"

"Not as good as I'd hoped."

Karl pulled onto the downtown street and started for Tower Heights. Adam stared out the window at the sidewalk, still vibrant with life, even though sunrise was quickly approaching.

Their route took them right alongside the heavily mosaicked walls of royal palace.

At this time of morning the figure of King Simon Columbain slaying the great serpent-demon seemed like it might almost spring to life. Soon the first morning rays would fall across the gilded tiles that comprised King Simon's sorcerous sword, Demonslayer. Adam admired the strength and courage of his forbearers in their historic deeds, but tried not to think about them too long. Ruminations of that sort would only lead him to fret over his own lack of heroic achievement. Better to admire King Simon and leave it at that.

As an attendant to his godmother, Lady Langdon, Adam's importance barely surpassed that of furniture. He looked good dressed in the West Court colors, yellow and gold. He had a nice voice. He could hold Lady Langdon's fur coat, handbag and hat simultaneously. He could play guitar and piano, but wouldn't unless asked. Other attendants had skills. Bankers. Accountants. Armies of lawyers to oversee the formal transfer of souls. Lady Langdon called upon them constantly. Him, she never needed for anything but to fetch and carry. This time, Grand Magician Drake of the Black Tower. Next time, maybe her umbrella.

Outside the downtown core, few cars moved, mostly delivery trucks entering the palace grounds, their square, dirty forms shabby against the polished rose marble walls.

Three soulless custodians, a thin, gray-haired man and two doughy women, finished polishing their section of wall and plodded across the entryway in a slow, silent procession. A truck driver didn't brake as he entered the palace gates, barely missing the last man. The soulless resumed polishing the wall, carefully scratching grime from the grout, sweeping the sidewalk and picking up cigarette butts from the gutter.

He saw Karl glance over at the soulless in the same searching way that inhabited animals seemed to.

"Looking for your old body out there?" Adam asked.

Karl shook his shaggy head and expelled a snort that Adam thought was much like laughter, then lifted one long-fingered hand and signed, "My body's dead, boss. Why do you think I'm inside of this monkey?"

"You could be a convict," Adam pointed out.

"Not with a palace chauffeur's license." Karl made a left up the hill toward the Tower Heights neighborhood, and then eased to a stop in the loading zone in front of a dark monolith of a building. He turned and pulled a huge orangutan grin and signed, "Here you go, boss, good luck in there."

It was not Drake's custom to be awake for any part of the morning, but on this occasion he happened to be observing the flowering of a new star low on the western horizon, and he was in a foul temper because of it. New stars, though rare, were a bother to the astrologically inclined, changing the whole meaning of the sky. They were also known to be harbingers of disaster so Drake examined it closely, speaking spells and taking measurements. He'd neither showered nor shaved for three days when his doorbell rang. His hair hung over his shoulders in greasy black strings. He stank.

Drake's servant, Nancy, appeared in his study doorway, dressed in her bathrobe and slippers. Her normally neat brown page-cut hair was so knotted and askew that it resembled a poorly kept and inexpensive wig.

"You have a gentleman caller from the West Court, sir. Lord—" She broke off, stifling a yawn. "Lord Adam Wexley."

"I'm not at home to guests," Drake snapped, then, turning away, murmured, "Nobles...they think they can ring your bell at any time of day they like."

"He says it's an emergency."

"Everything is an emergency for them. Send him away."

"He's got a nice smile," Nancy said. "And nice legs."

Drake left his telescope and crossed to the fishbowl that he used as a scrying device. On the water's surface, he conjured the image of his gentleman caller.

Lord Wexley was a tall rectangular man with very square shoulders and a casual looseness of his limbs that lent him a marionette-like appearance. He wore tight yellow and black club wear that looked tawdry in normal light. Drake could see Adam's small nipples through the sheer fabric. His eyes were blue.

"You say he said his business was of the utmost urgency?"

"No, I said he said he was here because of an emergency," Nancy corrected.

Drake waved the difference aside with an impatient hand.

"Bring our guest coffee. Tell him I will be with him as soon as I am able."

Drake showered and shaved and found a clean black shirt and a pair of jeans and put on his rings, malingering in the bath for as long as he could before joining his guest in the living room approximately an hour later.

Adam hadn't touched the coffee tray, apparently because he had fallen asleep.

He lay sprawled across Drake's bone-colored sofa like he owned it, smelling of whiskey, sweat and cigarettes. His short blond hair looked sticky with spent product. Drake sat in his armchair and poured himself some coffee. Drake expected Adam to wake, but he didn't. So Drake set the coffee pot down on its silver tray with an unnecessary clang. Nothing. Not even a snore. The grand magician leaned close to his ear.

"Lord Wexley, do you intend to spend the whole day asleep on my couch? I will expect you to pay me rent for it, I promise you."

Adam's bloodshot eyes popped open and he sat up, confused.

"Drake?"

"Yes, Lord Wexley?"

"Please call me Adam."

Drake nodded and Adam continued, "Grand Magician Zachary Drake, I wish to—"

"You wish to summon me to attend Lady Langdon, Minister of the West Court?"

"Yes, Lady Langdon—" he began, but Drake cut him off again.

"Certainly she must have told you that I prefer not to work for the Courts of the Four Directions," Drake said. Adam looked like a confused little boy who had just been told that the world is not flat after all, but can't quite grasp the information. His eyes roamed over Drake, as if he'd just noticed Drake had a physical presence.

Drake caught Adam's eyes lingering on his ostentatious and obviously magical rings. Drake sensed that he was rating them, deciding which ring looked most evil. Was it the blood diamond? The talon? The fat silver spider?

Drake wanted to reach out and smooth Adam's hair and straighten his collar. He restrained himself. He suspected that days spent doing nothing but mathematics had rendered him impulsive and delirious.

"But the astrologers have decreed that Lady Langdon's daughter Carolyn will be in labor before noon," Adam said as if this explained everything.

"I don't see how I could be of any use. I'm not well practiced in midwifery." Drake dropped a cube of cinnamon-sugar into his coffee.

"The Medallion of Rayner has been stolen. You must help get it back. Now do you understand?"

Drake understood immediately. Without Lady Langdon's holy medallion, the protective barrier surrounding her daughter would be incomplete, leaving mother and child vulnerable to curses and possession.

"That is unfortunate, but I must regretfully decline. Because of the appearance of a strange new star, I am currently engaged with remapping the night sky. It's a big project involving tricky mathematics that only I understand. I have no time to spare for finding Lady Langdon's lost jewelry." As Drake stood to leave, Adam caught him by the arm. Adam's hand felt warm from sleep.

"She knows where the medallion is, she just can't get it." Adam's cell phone rang again. He glanced at the display and looked pained. "Lady Langdon said that I must return with you at any cost, so name your price."

Drake considered asking Adam for either a kiss or his immortal soul but decided that the former gave his hand away and the latter... He had no use for a soul as pure as Adam's. But his earnest, guileless expression moved Drake. He thought that it was no wonder Lady Langdon had sent him. Adam fell well within Drake's tastes and usual strike range.

Crafty old biddy knows me too well, he thought. Aloud, he said, "Is that any way to beg my favor?"

Adam flushed deep red then bowed his deepest and most formal bow.

"I, Adam Wexley of the West Court, humbly request the honor of your presence in the court this morning, Grand Magician Drake. Would you please accompany me on this matter of great urgency?"

Drake smiled. "It would be my singular pleasure."

Though the sun had barely risen, Lord Thomas Myrdin of the South Court had already grown weary of arranging flowers. What did they matter? Louis had chosen Lady Carolyn for his consort and she would imminently bear him his child and heir. No man, no matter how ardent, could compete in that arena.

Still, the flowers had to be arranged and the poems had to be written lest the South lose its reputation as the most genteel of the Courts of the Four Directions. Already the other three nobles who shared his small garden courtyard were awake and performing their appointed tasks. Across from him on her own verandah, Lady Elizabeth Parker tuned her long-necked guitar. Because the lotus were blooming, she'd doubtless be brushing up on the seemingly endless song cycle "Ballad of the Lotus Princess" all day to honor the new princess when she came squalling into the world.

No escape from duty today, no matter how it pained him.

Before him lay an assortment of cut stems, pink roses, white nigella, and one massive red peony he regretted choosing. Though lovely and resplendent now, the flower would abruptly lose all its petals in a single hour, like the decorum suddenly falls away from a jilted woman in the midst of a nervous breakdown.

Or maybe not a woman.

He couldn't bear the thought of being present when that proud bloom fell to pieces. Still it had to be placed. Red peonies representing the South Court were prominently featured on their crest since time immemorial when the blood of King Simon Columbain fell upon a pure white peony forever staining it vermillion. This peony, named the Maura bloom after Myrdin's own ancestor, could never be passed over when in season. It was like a form of floral punishment.

Myrdin tried not to think of the parallels between himself and Maura Myrdin, the great suicidal consort to that first high king.

She, like himself, had been a virgin when she met the king. But unlike himself, she bore the next generation of sovereigns before committing herself to the noose, whereas he hadn't managed to replicate Louis's genetic material and was, therefore, a nonentity to be deleted from the annals of history. Even a dramatic suicide would bring him no lasting notoriety.

Myrdin accomplished his bouquet without pleasure and set the finished arrangement in the center of his room. After consulting the almanac, he chose a coil of fine incense correct for the day's ascending stars and set it alight. Fragrant smoke curled up through the cool morning light. Then he took out his painting set and started mixing colors.

To the outside observer, he appeared to be painting the just-groomed foliage, and this was mostly true. But anyone familiar with spells could have detected Myrdin's discreet words pressing magical commands into the paint.

Originally he'd spoken these illegal spells to ease the fortune of courtiers in the South Court, including himself, but more and more frequently, Myrdin spoke spells to calm his own anger. He manipulated the paintbrush expertly, allowing his heartache to be pulled out in long strokes. Once finished, like many of Myrdin's works, the painting would emanate sorrow and would have to be burned before its strange pathos came to the attention of any licensed magician. His art, like his existence, subtracted from history by the necessity of keeping it secret.

Myrdin's brush had been his locus of power even before his parents had been beheaded for treason, when he'd been a child attending the Royal Academy of Magic.

Before he met Louis.

A bell chimed and a red-robed page appeared in his doorway.

"Announcing Lord Roscoe, Minister of the South."

Myrdin set his brush aside, rose and bowed low as his adoptive father entered his suite, entourage in tow, nine attendants and an elderly terrier.

As usual, the dog rushed forward to greet Myrdin, tail wagging.

"Good morning, my lord, I had not expected such company so early in the day. I have nothing but fragrance to offer you." Myrdin gestured to the incense burner.

"Please take your seat." Lord Roscoe released Myrdin with a terse wave. The moment Myrdin sat back in his chair, the terrier jumped into his lap, where it preferred to stay. Myrdin petted it behind the ears, murmuring, "There's a good puppy."

Myrdin had never managed to learn either the dog's name or the name of the spirit who clearly inhabited her. Her collar read *Lord Roscoe's Prime Bitch*. Myrdin suspected he had one of his ex-wives locked up inside the canine. Roscoe took a certain pleasure in making the dog beg, which spoke volumes about his feelings toward the soul locked inside.

"The astrologers have foretold that His Majesty's daughter will be born today," Roscoe said.

"How delightful for him. I must write a congratulatory verse," Myrdin replied.

Lord Roscoe shook his head.

"You must take a delegation to the Malachite Palace at once to help form the protective barrier around Lady Carolyn as she births the heir." Lord Roscoe paced the room, pausing only to yank a yellowing petal out of one of the arranged roses. "Gregory will give you the South Court medallion." Roscoe indicated his lawyer with a vague wave.

"But I am not allowed to work magic." Myrdin felt the blood drain from his cheeks. "My mother's direct line is prevented for three generations, you know this."

"Protection rituals are exempt from prosecution," Gregory said. "You are the best candidate for keeping your strength for the duration."

"And I want your face to be among the supporters of Lady Carolyn, not conspicuously absent," Lord Roscoe put in. "I will not have it be whispered that the South Court is disloyal to the new princess."

"Yes, my lord." Myrdin bowed his head to hide his disgust at the thought of Lady Carolyn, good girl from a good family, but a tramp in Louis's bedroom.

Myrdin toyed with the ring on his hand. A pink sapphire. Louis had given it to him how long ago? Ten years at least. Just before his nineteenth birthday. He forced himself to stop these sentimental and nostalgic musings and face his adoptive father.

Lord Roscoe examined the flower arrangement again, seeming offended by it for reasons Myrdin could not discern.

"His Majesty has not been calling for your attendance much of late."

"His interest in drawing lessons has waned in recent months," Myrdin said.

"Do your best to see to it that he does not lose interest in art completely. We've all grown used to the benefits of His Majesty's favor." Without further preamble Lord Roscoe stood and walked toward the door. He'd said all he'd come to say.

"Thank you for the pleasure of your visit." Myrdin kept his tone elegant through sheer force of will. Lord Roscoe left without reply. One by one the attendants filed out behind him until only Gregory and the dog remained.

The lawyer opened his briefcase and removed an ancient golden box as long and wide as Myrdin's hand, but only a couple of fingers tall.

"The Medallion of Cleo." Gregory placed it on the table next to Myrdin's paintbrush. Sensing the power of the medallion, Myrdin's locus rolled slightly toward the box. Myrdin laid a casual hand atop his brush to stop it progressing farther. Gregory didn't notice, too busy shuffling through a stack of legal forms to pay attention. "I'll need you to sign this release."

Gregory produced a blood pen and deftly taped the needle end into Myrdin's hand. After pumping his hand a couple of times to fill the surgical tubing that fed the pen's nib, Myrdin signed the papers.

Gregory smiled, removed the pen from Myrdin's flesh and drained the remaining blood onto a cloth, which he returned to Myrdin as was polite, if slightly condescending. "Try not to lose the medallion. It's valuable."

Myrdin assured Gregory that he would not. Gregory departed, giving the terrier a sharp whistle as he stepped across

Myrdin's threshold. The dog gave Myrdin what he perceived to be a sympathetic look before trotting off after her master.

Myrdin straightened his robes and sent for his own attendants, three ladies and two lords to equal the lucky number six. While he waited he painted the peony, pressing his loneliness into the paint so that when his entourage arrived he felt blank as paper and well prepared for the coming ordeal.

Drake spent the drive to the palace looking at the back of Karl's hairy neck. The palace grounds were within easy walking distance of his Tower Heights home, but walking was an unacceptable way for a person of his rank to arrive at the palace. They drove through the crimson-tiled south gate and turned left, toward the West Court Palace. Few courtiers perambulated through the vast grounds at this time of morning, but servants abounded. Liveried gardeners wearing royal green pruned the hedge mazes. Maids dressed in South Court red scrubbed marble stairs, and porters carried cases of food or other goods into the South Court complex. Two minutes drive brought them to West Court. The maids washing these steps wore yellow. Karl stopped in front of Lady Langdon's residence where Lady Langdon's personal secretary hovered, waiting.

He ushered Drake into a large glass conservatory. The air was thick and humid with the vegetal smell of potted trees and pampered tropical flowers. Out of the corner of his eye, Drake spied a sulfur-crested cockatoo resting on a branch, watching. An inhabited animal, no doubt.

Adam's second wind had apparently kicked in. He charged forward, toward an older woman, who stood in the center of the room, looking up. Her dark hair was perfectly coiffed. Her suit, tasteful gold trimmed with chocolate, was immaculate. She held one high-heeled shoe in her hand and seemed to be preparing to hurl it at something.

"Lady Langdon, I've brought him!" Adam's shout startled the Lady and she almost dropped her shoe.

"Grand Magician, I'm so grateful." She put the shoe back on and shook Drake's hand. Her unadorned fingers looked dowdy against Drake's flamboyant display of rings.

"Mr. Wexley says that you're having some trouble this morning?"

"Too damn right I am. I need your help getting that down." She pointed at the ceiling.

Adam and Drake both looked up.

The Medallion of Rayner dangled in plain view, approximately twenty feet above Adam's head. It was clutched in the fearsome grip of an angry chimpanzee hunched in the top of a potted tree.

"Isn't that young Master Augustus's caddy?" Adam asked.

"He's called Charlie." Lady Langdon gave Drake a pleading stare.

"An inhabited animal?" Drake asked.

She nodded.

"Have you tried shaking the tree?" Adam laid a hand on the narrow trunk and Drake laid his hand on Adam's to stop him. Drake had no desire to antagonize the ape to retaliation. Though the soul that inhabited the body might be human, the encasing flesh still exerted strong animal tendencies. Feces would be flung.

Adam pulled his hand away, clearly too aware Drake's touch.

"When you shake it he just screams and jumps to another tree," Lady Langdon said. "I believe Charlie has been possessed by one of my rivals. Can you help?"

"Oh, certainly. Capturing fugitive simians is my specialty. I don't suppose you've considered simply darting him, have you?" Drake asked. "It would be fastest."

Before Lady Langdon could answer, Adam turned on Drake, his expression full of horrified reproach.

"He's inhabited," Adam said. "What if he falls? He feels pain."

"How thoughtless of me." Drake inclined his head, yielding to Adam's reflexive goodness. Drake noted that Lady Langdon failed to suppress a smug smile at the sight of his capitulation. "May I borrow your phone?"

While Drake made arrangements for what he would need, Adam talked quietly with Lady Langdon. When he glanced over to assess Drake's body, the magician pretended not to notice. Though Adam's eyes lingered appreciatively on Drake's long torso, Drake could tell that Adam disapproved of his ethics. No surprise there. Not many courtiers of his class would. Unaligned magicians were not the sorts of people a good boy could take home to mother. Drake waved at Adam, who returned a weak, unconvincing smile before suddenly needing to attend his mistress. He offered to play her a song on his guitar. She declined, which displeased Drake and not only because he thought it would positively influence the ape's temper.

Lady Langdon's other retainers arrived one by one, gradually forming a loose barricade of crisp yellow business suits around her. Doubtless these men and women helped run Langdon's banking empire, sedate and conservative as they were. Young and nocturnal, Adam stood out among their relentlessly displayed moderation.

The servants, mostly soulless human beings or inhabited animals, kept discreetly to the side or peeked around doorframes, waiting to be called.

Drake lit a cigarette and was immediately admonished for it by an older man in a fine butter-colored suit. Lady Langdon called him off. A few seconds later a soulless woman padded up, holding a large cut-glass ashtray for his use. When Drake paced, she followed behind.

At last the front bell rang. Nancy had arrived, trailed by another, more docile, chimpanzee. Drake crushed out his cigarette, knelt and whispered into the ape's ear.

"Please, everyone, come away," Drake said to the assembled retainers. "Margaret needs room to work."

"Margaret needs room?" Adam drifted toward Drake, his expression challenging; his lack of sleep manifesting as a lack of decorum. "I thought you were meant to retrieve the medallion."

"I am—in my own way." Drake smiled at Adam, though he was already watching Margaret climbing up the tree, calling out incomprehensible animal syllables to Charlie the caddy. "Even though Charlie is inhabited, he is still subject to the habits and longings of his body. He is still physically an ape and all apes long for the company of others."

Margaret sat in the crotch of the tree. Charlie screamed and bared his teeth.

"He doesn't seem to want Margaret's company," Adam said. "Maybe he doesn't like girls."

Adam's catty tone brought a perverse smile to Drake's lips.

"You shouldn't be so quick to attribute your own nature to others," Drake murmured, but not loud enough for the other retainers to hear. Louder, he said, "Those aggressions are the actions of the possessing spirit. Look into Charlie's eyes. He wants to be close to her. His flesh desires the comfort of one of his own kind, regardless of intellect or inhabiting spirit."

Drake gave Adam a long, unblinking stare and Adam rewarded him with a deep, confused flush. At that moment, Drake could see that though Adam didn't like him, he still wanted him.

Charlie suddenly dropped the medallion and climbed down the tree to be with Margaret. Lady Langdon's retainers dove for the medallion like a pack of well-pressed dogs scrambling after a single biscuit. She rushed for her car the moment the medallion fell into her hand, the barricade of suits unnecessarily clearing the way for her. Adam and Drake stayed behind in the conservatory, watching Margaret brush the leaves from Charlie's back.

Neither ape cared when Drake approached and laid his hand on Charlie's foot. The possessing spirit had fled the scene, but the fingerprint of the other magician remained flickering like an afterimage on Charlie's soul.

If Lady Langdon had been present, and had asked, Drake might have told her which magician had worked this possession against her, but she'd gone as soon as she had what she needed, so he declined to make an effort to inform her. Drake turned back to Adam.

"You see? In a battle of flesh and soul, flesh almost always prevails. This is just another example of how nobles are apt to automatically summon magicians when other professionals would be better suited to the job. In this case, I think you might have been better served by engaging a zookeeper." Drake removed another cigarette from his case. Adam surprised him by producing a lighter before Drake could find his own. As he leaned in to take the light, Adam gave him a look of such frank admiration that it was Drake's turn to look away. Drake wanted to lean forward and kiss Adam's throat and shoulders, to slide his hands down Adam's back, investigating the architecture of his muscles. Drake's ashtray-holder sidled up again, blankly. Her presence brought the magician back to his senses.

"My servant will stay here with Margaret for the day, until it's time for her to return to the Royal Menagerie. My work here is done."

"Thank you so much," Adam said. "I'm sure Lady Langdon extends her deepest gratitude."

"Gratitude, though lovely, is a little too intangible for me. I believe we need to settle on a payment, Mr. Wexley." Drake flicked ash into the crystal receptacle.

"Payment?" Adam pocketed his lighter, a wary expression on his face. "I guess we do."

"I would like you to play for me," Drake impulsively announced, the giddiness of sleep deprivation and minor triumph making him bold.

"My guitar?"

"Yes, I want you to play it for me."

"Right now?" The hoarseness of early morning roughened the edge of Adam's voice.

"On Saturday," Drake said, "at my penthouse in the Black Tower."

Adam swallowed, visibly nervous at the prospect, but he agreed.

Drake tried and failed to keep a satisfied smile from curling up from the corner of his lips. He couldn't help but relish this small victory. He hadn't had a date in a long time and although Adam's West Court remittance hardly qualified as a fully romantic appointment, he gloried in it all the same.

"I will look forward to the pleasure of your company then." Drake gave Adam a slight bow and swept out of the room in a sleep-deprived delirium.

Adam's orangutan driver took Drake home, giving him shifty glances the entire way, but Drake didn't mind. It was as much the nature of orangutans to be suspicious as it was Drake's to be the arrogant bastard who warranted it. Drake could not fault the beast.

Chapter Two

The Malachite Palace stood, monolithic in the center of the royal compound, surrounded by a labyrinth of hedges and fountains and bounded at the compass points by the Palaces of the Courts of the Four Directions.

The birthing chamber, where Myrdin and his entourage stood, chanting for nearly three hours already, was like a miniature version of the larger grounds. In the center of the vaulted stone room, an area had been curtained off with sheer green panels embroidered with the royal crest. Through these, Myrdin could dimly see Lady Carolyn in the birthing chair, surrounded by medical equipment as well as gowned nurses. The royal magical physician's stout form was easy to pick out, as well as the thin, spidery shape of the royal attorney.

Myrdin held the Medallion of Cleo in his hands while he and two of his attendants cycled their way through the spells of the protection ritual. He and the other courtiers would be here for the entire birth. Across the room Myrdin could see Arthur Drysdale-Martin, dressed in North Court purple. To Myrdin's right stood Samantha Bulltower, young Minister of the East in her modern blue business suit. Lady Langdon, mother of Lady Carolyn, grandmother of the future heir, had yet to arrive. In her place, Royal Magician Clifton Everett swayed and sweated, his white hair sticking out in uneven tufts around his ruddy, wrinkled face. He'd obviously been sleeping when Louis had sent for him. Where Myrdin, Drysdale-Martin and Bulltower each held a medallion, Everett held a pocket watch, his own locus of power. Together the four of them formed an imperfect barrier around Lady Carolyn, but it would hold against most magical attacks.

Louis had yet to make an appearance. Myrdin wondered if he and Lady Langdon were together. Strange alliance. Something must be going wrong.

The courtiers chanted on. When Myrdin's voice grew hoarse one or another of his attendants brought water, hot coffee, or a towel to wipe his face.

Myrdin felt a tremor pass through the air. The Medallion of Cleo grew hot in his hands.

The royal magician began to tremble and choke. Was he repelling a magical attack or experiencing myocardial infarction? Impossible to tell. Myrdin looked to Bulltower who didn't seem to have noticed the disturbance, but something was not right. If he let himself relax, Myrdin could see power being drawn from the three medallions represented as arcs of light. These arcs wove into the halo of spells protecting the baby and Lady Carolyn, and there was a gap—like a space where their chanting could not cover—a strange absence of light. Could no one else see this? He glanced at Everett. Surely the royal magician could see the deficiency and would act on it. But Everett looked as if he might collapse. Still chanting, Myrdin gestured for one of his attendants to see to the royal magician.

Just as the young woman pressed a glass of water to Everett's lips, the chamber doors opened and Lady Langdon rushed in, holding the Medallion of Rayner aloft. Everett relinquished his place, sagging against Myrdin's attendant as she and a boy from the North Court helped Everett to the edge of the chamber.

Again Myrdin felt a surge of heat pass through the Medallion of Cleo. Within each medallion lay the soul of one of the great magicians of antiquity, the brothers and sisters of Simon Columbain. United, these souls were invincible protection for the monarch. These very same medallions had protected Louis at his birth.

Now that all four medallions were present, Louis arrived to complete the spell. He stood in his place on the left side of the curtained bed, facing west to honor the court of his consort. Whispering, he rubbed his thumb across his emerald signet. He called forth the spirits of his ancestors. Arching light shot from the stones embedded in each of the medallions. The air grew close and hot. Myrdin shrugged off his outer robe and let it fall to the floor. He heard the squall of a newborn baby. Everett pushed himself up and approached the bed. The royal lawyer was already there. Though he could not see it clearly, Myrdin knew what was happening. The royal magician took blood from the heir's umbilical cord, gave it to the lawyer, who smeared it across a contract, which Lady Carolyn would sign. In this way, Louis would acquire the soul of his heir.

Proponents of this practice claimed that it kept the royal family from being owned by a foreign power. Myrdin, and almost every other courtier who was not delusional, understood that it was about control. No heir could usurp the throne, regardless of the age or incapacity of the monarch. Louis owned this baby's soul just as Lord Roscoe owned Myrdin's. That Lord Roscoe was, in turn, owned by Louis comforted Myrdin not at all. His days of enjoying the idea that he belonged to someone were long past.

Everett and the lawyer emerged seconds later, and Louis motioned for their chanting to cease. Myrdin gratefully accepted a cup of tea to soothe his throat while Louis looked over the contract.

After a minute, Louis smiled and held the contract aloft, grinning.

"It's a girl!" he shouted to Lady Langdon.

"Thank the Sea of Stars!" Lady Langdon said, tears streaming down her cheeks, tracing chalky pathways through her pressed powder.

For one moment, Myrdin thought of mentioning the gap he'd seen in the baby's defenses, but any admission of his understanding of magic would draw suspicion. No one would believe that he was an intrinsic, yet harmless magician. Not after his parents' execution. His gaze fell accidentally on Everett, and he found the royal magician's eyes boring into his with owlish intensity. Everett even cocked his head a little, regarding him in the sideways fashion of a bird. Myrdin looked away, glad that he had not become a magician after all. They all seemed to resemble their inhabited familiars too closely.

The East Court started a round of cheers, which were quickly seconded by the North Court and by Myrdin and his own entourage.

"Long live the princess!" he cried hoarsely, looking as happy as he could. "Long live Princess Julianna!"

Once the cheering died away, Myrdin replaced the Medallion of Cleo in its golden box and sent it, and his attendants, back to the South Court. Though he should have gone then, he found himself lingering in the antechamber anxious to congratulate Louis personally.

One by one the other courtiers drifted away until he was alone. He'd decided to give up and was gathering himself to leave when Clifton Everett emerged from the birthing chamber, flushed and puffing from exertion. Myrdin went to him immediately and helped the old man to a crushed velvet settee.

"Can I get you some water?"

"No, but something more medicinal would be a kindness," Everett said.

Myrdin smiled at Everett's hopeful expression. He went to the sideboard where Louis kept his whiskey. He felt Louis would have offered the man a drink, had he been in the room, so he played host and poured the royal magician two fingers. Everett drank it in three fast gulps and fell back on the settee. He eyed Myrdin.

"I must say, Lord Myrdin, after watching your stamina I find it a tragedy that you are prohibited from practicing more magic."

"You mean the ritual? That's not magic." Fear zinged through Myrdin.

"The protection ritual is still a spell, is it not?" Everett raised an eyebrow.

"Yes, but it can be done by anyone holding the medallion. It's not real magic."

"But the energy you fed into the spell wasn't coming from the medallion—at least not all of it. It was coming at least partially from you. Some star smiles down on you and lends you her light. Magic can't get more real than that. Tell me, do you have prophetic dreams?"

"Only in the way that any dream could be called prophetic." Myrdin brushed the topic aside. "Tell me, do you favor the whiskey?"

Everett regarded Myrdin and seemed to recognize for the first time how uncomfortable the conversation was making him. "The whiskey is excellent. I can see that my conversation displeases you, my lord. Fear not, I'll keep my thoughts about your powers to myself. The law is the law."

"Exactly so." Myrdin's relief emanated from the center of his chest. He made a shallow bow. "I'm afraid I must excuse myself, Royal Magician."

"Certainly, but—" Everett caught hold of Myrdin's sleeve and pulled him close, whispering, "I know of only one star whose light shines with opal fire like that."

"The Guardian Star?" Myrdin whispered.

"The very same!"

Noise from approaching courtiers made Myrdin leap back. He left the antechamber without taking leave of Everett, heart constricted with yearning. Could it really be true? No, he decided as he wound through the labyrinth of hedges back to the South Court. Everett was old and most likely going senile. He was mistaken. The only opalescent light he'd seen was the light refracting through the fingerprints on his own glasses. It was Myrdin's own fatigue making Everett's insane idea seem momentarily plausible.

By the time he collapsed, still in full archaic robes, onto his bed, he'd put Everett from his mind.

Adam announced his mission—performing a private recital for Grand Magician Drake—to nearly every one of his godmother's retainers. He'd received reactions from them ranging from sympathetic amusement to amused sympathy. Only Lady Langdon herself seemed to understand the importance of his action. She gave him leave to excuse himself from all duties and court functions (except for the party to honor Lady Carolyn and the Princess Julianna) in order to practice.

The night of the party found him on the West Court Palace verandah, slouched between the tall marble pillars that faced the Malachite Palace, playing his guitar. He looked out past the vast labyrinth of the king's gardens to the royal residence, shrouded tonight and every night in a distorting haze of protective spells.

Behind him, inside the West Court Palace, the party was in full swing. A buffet was set out with tablecloths in royal green and West Court yellow. Courtiers drank white wine or absinth and ate shrimp and laughed, swapping snapshots of their own babies before settling into conversations about money.

Congratulations abounded for Lady Langdon's new rank—the next queen's grandmother. Adam felt happy for her and proud to be in her retinue but also out of place with the financial set. They were strange and threatening to Adam. Secretive. Calculating. Always keeping one eye on the door in a way that Adam would never do. He imagined that their vigilance was for Lady Langdon's sake. He imagined they admired his bravery and resourcefulness in procuring the services of an unaligned and notoriously recalcitrant magician. Pride welled in him, as he practiced the songs he would play for Grand Magician Drake, at the thought that he would finally perform a substantive duty for his godmother. Not as heroic as slaying a demon, perhaps, but still useful.

The full moon shone down on the summer night. Guests came and went, mostly mistaking him for an antisocial musical savant. Near three a.m., when the party had quieted to candid murmurs and drunken confessions, a handsome man ambled out onto the veranda. He seemed preoccupied, his straight blond hair falling unnoticed into his eyes.

Adam noted him, absently. His red linen suit identified him as a member of South Court and his long, old-fashioned hairstyle communicated high rank. He gazed out across the labyrinth, swirling his absinth. He toyed with a large pink sapphire ring on his pinkie.

He looked so handsome and so sad that Adam immediately wanted to try and cheer him.

"Can I play you a song, Lord Sapphire?" Adam asked. The man started in confusion.

"Are you speaking to me?"

"Is there anyone else here?" Adam didn't mean his words to sound harsh, but they did and so he tried to soften them. "Certainly there's no one else who deserves to be named for such a beautiful jewel. So tell me what song I can play for you tonight."

"All right," he said. "Do you know 'One Moonlit Night'?"

"This one?" Adam plucked out the first few notes. It was an old song from the days of Queen Rexella. Every first-year guitar student learned it. Adam had expected a more modern request from Lord Sapphire. He'd also expected the man to provide his real name, so that Adam could introduce himself but since Lord Sapphire declined to correct Adam's presumptuous renaming, Adam decided to continue on in anonymity.

"Yes, that's the one."

"It's such a sad song." Adam, who had never liked the tune, loved the lyrics even less and couldn't imagine that the sound of it would bring cheer to another person.

"The song is not sad," Lord Sapphire said. "The inevitable truth of the temporal nature of all love is sad. I prefer to think of the song as merely honest."

"Just as you say." Adam sang all three depressing verses describing the forbidden love, betrayal and eventual suicide of the famous concubine, Maura Myrdin. As he sang, Adam wondered why anyone would bother to commit such a pointless story to verse, let alone put it to music.

After he finished, Lord Sapphire stayed silent for a long time. Then he said thank you, dumped his absinth over the edge of the veranda and started down the stairs toward the sidewalk. Adam stared after him with intense longing, both physical and sympathetic. He imagined himself chasing after Lord Sapphire, catching him and embracing him in the moonlight. He pictured himself demanding that the other man accept the comfort of his arms and forget all his sadness. He set aside his guitar and stood, only to discover that he'd waited too long, and Lord Sapphire had disappeared along the dark and twisting paths of the palace grounds.

Drake had been invited to the celebration for Princess Julianna, but had declined the invitation out of general dislike for both babies and conversations about banking.

He spent the evening of the Lady Langdon's party downtown on the rooftop patio of the Opal Room. He didn't normally go to the Opal Room because he disliked private clubs, even ones that he was a member of, and also because the Opal Room usually contained at least five too many magicians per square yard for him to feel completely comfortable there. It was the only place, though, that he could go to discuss his theories with Clifton Everett, his colleague and mentor.

Like most astrologer-magicians, Everett planned their meeting according to the favorable ascension of stars. That night 7:12 was the auspicious time and that was when Everett sat down. Perfectly punctual, as always. As he seated himself, a servant brought Everett's favorite whiskey, Phoenix single malt, and two glasses before silently withdrawing in fearful deference.

Everett wore thick glasses with bifocals and an old blazer bearing the crest of the Royal Academy of Magic, Drake's own alma mater. His thin white hair was combed neatly back. Like most other magicians of his generation, he wore no rings or any other jewelry, but sported an old and complex pocket watch that he used as a locus for his power. Being a friend of Drake's father, Everett had taken up a paternal attitude toward Drake after an accident rendered the senior Drake incapable of maintaining his parental role. He'd also married Drake's late mother, presumably for the same reason, but that was long after Drake had left the nest.

"I suppose you want to talk to me about the new star?" Everett spoke without preamble—a habit acquired from years of teaching.

"If my calculations are correct then I believe this may be the Ghost Star."

"I absolutely agree." Everett poured a shot of whiskey from his bottle and offered one to Drake, who politely declined. He'd already had one glass of wine and was wary of getting too drunk in a room full of soul snatchers. One slip of the tongue and he could end up living the rest of his days peering at the ankles of the world through the eyes of a terrier while his body gathered cigarette butts from the palace gutters.

It had, after all, happened to his father in this very establishment. Drake had seen his father three times since then and only from afar.

"Have you ever seen the Ghost Star before?" Drake asked.

"When I was twenty-six years, three months and seven days old the material and spectral planes came into conjunction and the Ghost Star appeared on the southern horizon. Not much came of it. A few restless souls made it out of the grave. Nothing else." Everett paused, apparently assessing Drake.

33

Then he leaned close, speaking softly so as not to be overheard. "At that time no magician was insightful enough to understand the opportunities afforded by a conjunction of this kind. When our world and the demon world are at their closest point, a shadow eclipse occurs. Our sun goes dark and the light of the Ghost Star becomes intense. Spectacular magics can be accomplished when the barrier between the realms is thin and permeable."

Everett's remarks immediately aroused Drake's suspicion. "I suppose if I had need of spectacular magic, I would be considering the possibilities. But sadly I tend to confine myself to more mundane pursuits."

Everett smiled ruefully. "I suppose we all do what satisfies us. But I will tell you that if a more ambitious magician were to want to free an owned soul, say one that currently resided in a lapdog, the conjunction would be the time to move without repercussions."

Drake could not look at his former teacher, lest his resentment become too obvious for even Everett's weak eyes to miss. He thought, *If you wanted to free my father's soul, why not do it yourself? Why incite me to break laws of ownership?*

"Ambition is not a vanity I've ever been accused of," Drake said. "Though I certainly wouldn't try to stand in the way of anyone else's dreams of glory."

Everett let out a snort of defeated laughter before murmuring, "Well spoken, Zachary. You are, as always, untainted by aspirations above your station. Speaking of your station, have you considered Madame Gantry's request? She can't keep working forever, you know. She barely fended off last winter's flood gales. A new Guardian of the City must take her place."

"I chose to decline her appointment." Drake scowled. He hated being called by his given name. He especially hated when Everett called him by his given name in that particular tone of paternal reproach. "I cannot assume her office."

"You won't, you mean." Everett sighed and gazed out over the spires and skyscrapers of the city.

"All right then, I won't. The Guardian Star has never risen in my constellation and according to my calculations, never will."

"Your magical skills are more than adequate to the task." Everett poured himself another whiskey.

"I am not chosen," Drake insisted. "I've checked. I've done the math and I know I'm not wrong. I told Madame Gantry that I would help her find the new guardian, but I would not take over her duties. I've been figuring the Ghost Star into our previous astrological projections, and I think I have an idea where the new guardian was born, so that should narrow the search."

"Not by much. We've been searching for the new guardian for decades without success. We were testing students when you were in your first year at the academy."

"Wanting me to be the guardian won't make it true," Drake said. "I know it would be easy, but I am simply not the chosen guardian. I'm sorry."

"All right, forget the Guardian Star. What about the Ghost Star? Have you reworked your horoscope to factor the influence?"

"I have. All signs point toward upheaval," Drake said. "What else?"

Everett nodded to himself, his attention drawn by the glittering city beneath them. Drake watched as well, aware of the dangers that could befall the great metropolis should she be left without a guardian in the time of need. Magic held the city together. It kept the fault lines from slipping and kept the sea from swallowing her in winter. Magic kept the citizens from turning on each other in savage tribal riots.

For twelve generations, some magician had felt the call to sacrifice their freedom for the glory of their great city. Much as it would have pleased his mentor, Drake knew that that guardian would not be him.

When Madame Gantry had started to pressure him, Drake had made a habit of tracking the movements of the Guardian Star through the constellations. He knew, for example, that the guardian had been born and was near his own age. He or she was, unlike Drake, the descendant of a noble house, though legitimacy was anyone's guess. Most importantly, the guardian would feel the call, which Drake did not. He felt, if anything, an active repulsion at the idea of giving himself to civil service.

Everett had grown distracted, squinting into the setting sun. "Excuse me, for a moment, will you? My familiar's having trouble with a scalper's web. She flew too close to the hospital and got stuck."

"They're getting quite bold, aren't they?" Drake commented. "We should talk about it at the next meeting of the Academy of Magic."

"Indeed." Everett stood and walked to the rooftop railing, peering out intently at the skyline, past the vast green expanse of the palace grounds to the eastern horizon, jagged with snow-topped White Mountains. He drew a slim telescope from his inside jacket pocket and gazed out toward the hospital. Had it been another magician working a spell to free his familiar's soul from a scalper's web, Drake might have offered assistance. But this was Everett. He needed no intervention.

Drake toyed with his empty wine glass, wishing there was something in it. He didn't need the liquor. He just wanted a handy reflective surface so that he could indulge in his newest hobby—spying on Adam Wexley. Every time he felt the childish grip of infatuation closing around his heart, he told himself that he was no longer the sort of pervert who would surreptitiously peer into the mundane life of a pathetic crush. And every time he made himself a liar. Adam was no exception. Earlier in the evening, while waiting for Everett to arrive, he had watched Adam showering and dressing for Lady Langdon's party. He watched Adam merely wash, completely failing to curl his hand around his own shaft, gently toy with his nipple rings or engage in any other private masturbatory act. It was disappointing but for the best, considering Drake was sitting in the middle of the Opal Room in broad daylight.

Now the urge to watch struck again, intensely, and he found himself pouring two fingers of whiskey into an empty lowball glass. He ran the jewel of his blood diamond around the edge and Adam's image appeared. He was playing his guitar.

"Sorry about that." Everett's voice drew Drake out of his voyeuristic trance. He tapped the side of the glass with his ring and Adam's image vanished, though not fast enough for Everett to miss it. "Decided to have a little whiskey after all then?"

"Just this once," Drake said.

Everett reseated himself. On his shoulder was the cockatoo from the previous morning.

"Sandy said she saw you in the West Court yesterday." Everett fed the bird a pellet that he'd fished out of the pocket of his blazer. "You aren't considering relinquishing your unaffiliated status are you?"

"Never. It was only a freelance job."

"You should be careful of doing anything for the West Court. Langdon has far-reaching plans," Everett said.

"For me?"

"Not for you. Not that I know of, anyway. But she's not the sort of person who misses an opportunity so it's best not to give her one." Everett's gaze flickered down to Drake's whiskey glass.

"I assure you that I have no inclination to ally myself with anyone in any court."

"That's good to hear." Everett picked up his own glass, causing Sandy to squawk a complaint. "To magic, free of politics."

"To magic," Drake replied.

Magic.

It, like everything else of value, had been taken from him early.

Myrdin often dreamed of his three years at the academy. He'd been a lackluster student, drawing through all of his classes, showing no stunning aptitude. He'd never approached the feats of excellence managed by Zachary Drake, the child prodigy one year his junior.

But he had loved it.

When he dreamed, his lips moved through the simple spells that he had learned: seek, protect, hide.

In his dreams he painted sanctuaries, quiet places of beauty. With the opal light of a benevolent star, he painted safety into his world.

This night his sanctuary was full of crying. A baby squalled in the distance, growing louder and louder, eroding the light. Each cry drew a veil of dark clouds across the night sky.

Red light pulsed from a single point in the clouds, shining down on Princess Julianna. Flames curled through the air around her. Dread overcame him.

Was this an omen?

But when he opened his eyes, the reality of the dream faded. How ludicrous. How needlessly dramatic of his subconscious to imbue Princess Julianna with dreadful powers.

But then the royal magician had asked him about prophetic dreams. Could this have been real?

He slid from bed and found a light cotton robe. Red, of course. He thought, as he often did, that he should buy some modern clothes now that he no longer attended the king so closely. He should follow the lead of that guitar player from the West Court. Cut his hair, take an interest in the world outside the palace walls, meet men for whom he was not required to write poetry daily.

Hope glimmered through him as he imagined himself leaving the palace and starting a new life. But Lord Roscoe would call him back. Lord Roscoe owned his soul and would never let him buy it back as long as Louis had even the smallest shred of interest in him. Already Lord Roscoe planned to install him as the princess's art and poetry teacher—an auspicious appointment that kept South Court in the sphere of influence. Every day he would be required to school the girl in the finer points of courtly life.

Suddenly, he could not endure the thought of that fate.

He would go to Louis and beg to be relieved of these duties. Louis couldn't refuse him that, could he? Not after all this time? Without bothering to put on his shoes, Myrdin set out through the labyrinth toward the Malachite Palace.

He threaded his way through the darkness, skirting the enormous statue of Queen Rexella that marked the halfway point. Though the labyrinth was deserted at this time of night, a sulfur-crested cockatoo sat on the statue's bronze shoulder. Myrdin paused, staring up at it. No bird should be awake at this hour, much less staring down at him. A magician's aura surrounded it.

"Who are you?" he demanded. The cockatoo flapped its wings and flew down.

"Sandy," the bird croaked. "Familiar of Royal Magician Everett. He sends his greetings."

"What do you want?"

"I've been watching over you." Sandy flapped her wings again and shook her head so that the yellow feathers waggled back and forth. "You are a great magician."

"I am not!" Myrdin hissed. "Leave me alone."

"But the city needs you. There may come a time when every citizen will need your protection. It will be your duty to keep them safe down to the last lark and pigeon."

"What are you getting at?" Myrdin said. "Speak plainly."

"The next Guardian of the City has still not been found, though his star began to burn twenty-nine years ago. How old are you, my lord?" Sandy laid a taloned foot on Myrdin's arm.

"You can't be serious," Myrdin said.

"The law is not stronger than fate and if the Guardian Star has chosen you, you must answer her call, whatever the cost."

"You're mad!" Myrdin pulled his sleeve from the cockatoo's claw. "I was already tested in school. I'm not the guardian."

"All tests are fallible," Sandy said. "I won't trouble you any further, but if you are ever in need of anything, hang a red sash in the window and I will come to you."

"This is just insane." Myrdin pulled his robe closer around him, suddenly realizing that he was in his pajamas in the labyrinth talking to a strange bird. "I'm going to talk to Louis."

He ran the rest of the way to the Malachite Palace and mounted the broad steps with the same speed that he'd been able to muster when he was a teenager. Except then enthusiasm, rather than panic, had fueled his haste.

The guards recognized him and let him pass through the great doors and run up the inside staircase to Louis's suite. He waited while Louis's chamber servants announced him, trying not to feel self-conscious when they looked down at his bare, dirty feet.

"The king would be happy to receive you, Lord Myrdin." The chamber servant bowed low. Myrdin rushed through the door. Louis reclined on an emerald velvet couch, his hand resting gently on the head of a young man in North Court purple who was sucking Louis's cock. The young man glanced up at Myrdin, then back down, cheeks reddening in embarrassment.

"Thomas!" Louis smiled indulgently. "Come join us."

The sight did not shock Myrdin. It had occurred with such frequency over the last decade that he'd become inured to jealousy and only experienced a certain relief that someone was already performing a duty that Myrdin himself had acquired an aversion to. But it meant Louis was in no mood for conversation.

"I need to talk to you about your daughter." He kept his eyes on Louis's, ignoring the gentle bobbing of the North Court man's head.

"You'll be her teacher, don't worry. Come, sit down. You should give Anthony a try. You don't mind, do you, Anthony?"

Anthony released his lip lock on Louis's dick long enough to murmur, "No, Your Majesty," before once more engaging the royal member.

"I'm sure Anthony is amazing, but this is important," Myrdin said. "It's about a bad omen."

"Have you been having nightmares again?" A hint of annoyance crept into Louis's tone. Myrdin recognized it, feared it, as Louis slid easily from irritation to rancor to hostility. "Take your medicine and go back to bed. If you still feel clairvoyant in the morning tell me then."

"You don't understand, Louis, tomorrow might be too late! Your daughter will bring a demon into the world."

Anthony stopped sucking. He lifted his head and stared at Myrdin like he was completely insane, then, as if a sudden thought had struck him, he began to snicker.

"I think this is called a cry for attention, Your Majesty," he whispered. Louis smirked and ran a thumb over Anthony's shiny bottom lip before pushing his head back down.

"Back to business, you." Louis ruffled Anthony's hair affectionately before turning his attention to Myrdin. "This is just pathetic, Thomas. Don't embarrass yourself this way."

"But I had a vision."

"Don't try my patience." An angry tone edged Louis's voice and Myrdin instantly dropped the subject.

"Yes, Your Majesty." Myrdin bowed low enough to catch Anthony's eye. The young man actually smirked at him.

Myrdin did as he was told.

He returned to South Court and, seeking oblivion, he took two sleeping pills.

But this night and the three nights following, he only managed to force himself back into the same dream.

Louis writhed, skin slick with blood, cells ruptured by walls of piercing sound.

And the city burned. Sheets of fire and screaming flowed down the streets like water. The air above black and thick with souls trapped between life and death.

The child will bring a demon into the world.

Myrdin felt it with absolute clarity. She had to be stopped.

Rising, drenched with sweat on the fourth night, he found his red sash and hung it in the window.

Minutes later the cockatoo appeared.

"What can I do for you, Lord Myrdin?" she croaked.

"I've had the dreams. The princess will bring the end of this city. Something must be done. Please tell the royal magician I need his help."

Sandy returned three hours later, holding a small bundle in its talons, which it dropped on the ground at Myrdin's feet. Inside the folded silk he found an antique stopwatch, a small vial of white crystals and a sheaf of papers.

"I'm glad you've decided to embrace your destiny," the bird said in its strange, squawking voice. "Instructions for what must be done are contained in the letter."

"And this?"

"Cocaine." Sandy cocked her head on the side. "In case you need some extra energy. We cannot meet again. It would be too dangerous."

"I understand." Myrdin secreted the items in his sleeve. "May the Sea of Stars shine on you."

"And on you." The bird took flight, a white mark on the inky black sky.

43

Still tormented by his nightmares—no, visions—Myrdin went to the moon pool. There he found the old terrier sitting on the edge of the pool gazing at itself in the water.

The dog looked up at his approach and Myrdin extended his hand. The terrier leaned against him, and suddenly the dog's servitude and derogatory collar seemed like too much of an insult for any soul to bear. Whatever this dog had done to Lord Roscoe, it had more than made amends. He held the dog, petted it and looked into its eyes, speaking to the human locked inside.

"Do you want to get out of here?"

The dog nodded and wagged its tail.

Myrdin gathered up the dog and walked to the edge of the palace grounds, past the guards and across the busy street. Then he bent and removed the offensive collar.

"Go on now. You're free."

Chapter Three

Adam had spent the past week constructing wild and romantic dreams of his next meeting with the forlorn Lord Sapphire. Even when riding the elevator up to Drake's penthouse, Adam pondered what Lord Sapphire's elevator was like. He thought that it probably was not as dull.

He did not remember the elevator at the Black Tower being so average. The wormwood paneling, which he'd previously found threatening, now merely looked like wood. The buttons, one through thirteen, glowed a friendly, rather than sinister, orange. He pressed the button for the thirteenth floor, the one that led to the grand magician's penthouse, with none of the trepidation that he'd previously experienced. He felt good. The West Court was ascending in power and Lady Langdon had hinted very strongly that she might be considering raising his allowance.

As he lifted his hand to press the intercom, Drake's voice burst out of the tiny speaker.

"Good evening, Lord Wexley."

"Good evening, Grand Magician." Adam found himself bowing out of reflex, even though he was alone in the elevator.

"Please come up." The elevator started to rise. Although this seemed to be a purely mechanical operation, Adam wondered if it might be magical after all and started to feel a little nervous. When the elevator doors opened into a tiny foyer containing two potted plants and Grand Magician Drake's front door, Adam's heart raced.

As Adam raised his hand to ring the bell, the door sprang open. Adam yelped and dropped his guitar case, which emitted a weird twanging noise.

"I'm sorry." Drake stepped back from the doorway. "I didn't mean to startle you."

"I just didn't expect you to answer so fast." Adam picked up his guitar case. "Actually, I didn't expect you at all. What happened to your servant?"

"She has the night off." Drake stepped aside and Adam came in, glancing around the great room as though he'd never stepped foot inside before. He didn't remember anything about Drake's condo except that he had a comfortable couch and a servant called Nancy.

Drake's condo had a 360-degree view of the city. Two of his living room walls were vast windows that displayed his roof garden. The sun was just setting, firing the sky in shades of mauve and cantaloupe. The city lights were beginning to wink on in the surrounding high-rises. Heavy, bone-colored curtains were drawn open, letting in the fading light. Oddities filled the largely black and white room, the most eye-catching being a curio cabinet filled with articulated skeletons as well as many fishbowls. Empty fishbowls. Also, shallow, dark-colored dishes of water. Adam wondered what they were for. Something magical, no doubt.

Adam found himself looking for Nancy, then remembered that she had gone.

"Do you ever wonder what soulless people do on their nights off?" Adam asked.

"Try in vain to locate that missing part of themselves now residing in a helpful bonobo?" Drake laughed. Adam didn't care for his flippancy.

"Have you ever asked your servant where she goes?"

"What convinces you that my servant is soulless?" Drake asked.

"Isn't she?"

"Not at all."

"I guess she just had a really blank expression when I saw her before." Adam felt his cheeks reddening. "She probably wouldn't be happy to know I thought she was soulless."

"It was five o'clock in the morning last time you met. I think she would most likely agree that she appeared to lack spiritual fire. But since you asked, she told me she was going to stay at her sister's place in the suburbs. Beyond that I don't know her plans." Drake walked to the sliding glass door that led to his roof garden. "I thought that we could sit on the patio."

In the distance, the vast, dark quadrangle of the royal palace and grounds cut its archaic form into the bustling city. Adam looked toward it with longing. He wondered what Lord Sapphire was doing right at this minute, then remembered himself and turned a polite smile on Drake.

Drake offered him a drink; Adam asked for seltzer.

"I don't think I've ever met a magician who has a human servant before," Adam remarked.

"No, I don't think there are many who do," Drake replied. "Magicians are, if nothing else, deeply paranoid. A free-willed human can't be trusted."

"But you trust your servant, don't you?"

"We have a mutual understanding." Drake's tone was noncommittal.

"Then she's your concubine?" Adam asked.

"Concubine? I shudder at the mere thought of having any kind of sex with Nancy. No, I came across her soul about seven years ago. At the time she inhabited a racing greyhound. The man who'd purchased her was selling off his menagerie to pay off a debt. It took a little while for me to locate her body. Finally, I found her at a day-labor agency. Once I had the two, putting them back together was relatively easy."

"And the greyhound?"

"She kept the greyhound until he passed away. He was an elderly creature who did nothing but sleep on her bed all day." Drake sat down in the chair next to him. Warm night breezes carried the scent of blooming jasmine over them. "She was very fond of the dog, having once shared a body with him."

"So you still own her soul, you just let her keep it inside her body?" Adam had never heard a story like this and was having trouble grasping it. Certainly, Lady Langdon would never have been so lax about enforcing loyalty.

"No, I rescinded my rights to it. We have a wage-payment agreement, as they do in the civil sector."

"If you don't own souls how do you power your magic?"

"I didn't say that I don't own souls. I just don't own her soul. I seek out the worst, lowest, most violent and cruel people I can find. Those are the souls I keep locked inside my rings where they are bereft of body and can do no harm without my command. But I didn't invite you here to listen to me talk about magic." An edge of businesslike callousness sharpened Drake's tone. "I invited you here to play."

"Of course." Adam opened his guitar case and felt his expression collapse. One string was broken. "I didn't bring any extra."

"I won't mind if you play without one," Drake said amicably.

"You want me to play without a string?" Adam searched his brain for a way to explain to Drake that the polyphonic music of the guitar made this task awkward and difficult. Then another thought occurred. Was this a test? Had Drake somehow witched a broken string on his guitar to see what he was really made of? So he said, "All right."

As Adam tuned his instrument, Drake stared up at the darkening sky. Adam watched Drake's face cycle through a series of baffling expressions as he fixedly glared at the night sky. He wondered uneasily about Drake's temperament and made his voice very gentle.

"Grand Magician?"

"Drake will do."

"Is there anything you'd like to hear?" Adam asked.

"I leave it to you," Drake replied.

"Should I sing?"

"If you want."

"I'd prefer to just play."

"Then just play."

Adam started to play the song he'd played for Lord Sapphire, wondering again why the other man had chosen it. To a Rexellan courtier, suicide loomed large in the list of possible solutions for the pain of unrequited love. Other popular options included contracting a wasting illness or becoming a vengeful demon and raining destruction down on the city. He couldn't imagine Lord Sapphire doing any of those things. He looked too noble to be brought low.

Adam played for about half an hour, always having to move his fingers into awkward configurations.

Then the doorbell rang. Adam glanced at the door and back at Drake, who was ignoring the sound. He was well used to ignoring visitors from attending Lady Langdon during her frequent headaches.

"Your hands must be tired," Drake said.

Adam looked up and caught a hesitant, but definitely sensual smile playing across the other man's lips. The idea that the magician had a sexual interest in him began to form in his mind. Unlike the other magicians he'd met, Drake's face was not inscrutable. To him, Drake seemed almost shy, although how that could be possible was a mystery.

"They are a little tired." Adam set his guitar aside and focused his attention on his host. He still looked as scary as ever. Slim black shirt and trousers. Boots with silver filigree tips. Silver rings. But now Adam noticed a subtle cologne, the glossiness of his hair. His smooth jaw.

Drake had shaved for him. Adam could see that his direct attention made Drake nervous because that hesitant look returned.

Suddenly Adam found himself in much more familiar territory. Indeed, he began to consider the possibility that guitar playing was not the activity that Drake most hoped Adam would engage in during his visit to the Black Tower. This changed everything.

While he was good at playing guitar, Adam's true excellence resided in the area of lovemaking. He smiled and offered his hands to Drake who took them, sliding his own long, thin fingers across the surface of his palms.

The doorbell rang again. And again. It rang at one-second intervals for a half-minute.

Drake's face revealed his emotions. First, that he definitely wanted to continue to explore more of Adam's skin, and second, that he was annoyed by the doorbell and that Adam should do something about it.

"Would you like me to tell them to go away?" Adam asked.

"Since my servant is away, thank you," Drake said. Adam stood and pressed the button for the elevator intercom.

"Grand Magician Drake is not accepting guests this evening." When he lifted his thumb off the button, the only sound to come through the speaker was a barrage of barking. He looked to Drake who immediately ran his diamond around the rim of his glass. The crystal glass sang out that clear, resonant note that directly precedes shattering. A fresh round of barking drowned out the sound.

Adam turned back, in bewilderment, to the speaker.

"I'm going to have to ask you to leave." As he spoke Adam heard Drake's glass shatter.

"Don't send him away!" Drake ran from the patio and slammed his hand onto the oval button that started the elevator moving up. Adam stepped back from Drake, baffled by the sudden reversal. Drake smiled at him in what looked like a feeble attempt at reassurance. "I believe I know that dog."

Drake pulled the front door open and lunged into the foyer. The lighted display above the elevator indicated the car had reached the tenth floor, then the eleventh.

Drake's expression was one Adam had never seen outside a movie theater—a sort of agony of hope.

Adam's only thought was that Drake was not the sort of man who he'd imagined as having such an intensely emotional relationship with a dog, and by the sound of the bark, a small one. He could see Drake having affection for an albino python, maybe, or a raven. But to Adam, love of a cuddly pooch did not jibe with Drake's spider-shaped ring. The thought that he might have judged another man's character on fashion accessories alone generated a grimy, shallow shame in Adam. Briefly, the notion crossed Adam's mind that the dog was inhabited, but by who?

An ex-lover? Certainly the expression on Drake's face communicated the importance of the dog, whoever it was.

Whoever it was, he wouldn't be happy to find Adam here, certainly.

This evening should be over, he thought, and aloud he said, "Perhaps I should go," but the grand magician didn't answer.

Above the elevator the number thirteen lit up and the doors slid open.

Thomas Myrdin could not rest.

It hadn't been his plan, but he had been unable to sleep without being afflicted by images of armies of soulless marching through the streets. Burning and silent, dropping limply to the ground as fire consumed them. Tired, he took a tiny scoop from the vial of cocaine Everett had provided and regained his feeling of alertness.

He had to act!

No, he had to wait. The timing was very specific. At 10:15 on the mark he should begin.

Myrdin dipped his paintbrush in red ink and drew, on the palm of his right hand, a butterfly and on his left hand, a peony. He waited while the ink dried, still as a statue, watching the minutes tick by on the clock. Five hours to go. He did his hair, chose his finest robe and jewelry, wrote a long, explanatory letter to Louis. Still three hours.

He soon tired of pacing the confines of his chambers. He'd gone to the moon pool, trying to find meditative contemplation in its glassy surface, but he could not.

Myrdin toyed incessantly with the watch, turning it over in his hand. It was set for eighteen seconds. That's how long of a window he had to penetrate the defenses surrounding the baby girl. The instructions were simple, ridiculously so.

Loop one end of the chain around her throat, and the other around your wrist. Hit the button.

Some part of him still rebelled against the act he must commit—to kill an infant—it was monstrous. But the compulsion inside him to save the city was stronger. The thought of protecting all those other people filled him with the opal light, transcended guilt and remorse and pain. He would sacrifice his honor for them. Even if they never knew it, this, his last unthinkable action, would save them all.

The elevator doors slid open and Drake rushed forward with reckless haste that he'd always been told was dangerous in a grand magician. Drake fell to his knees as the brown and white terrier walked out of the elevator and sat down in front of him. Her tail thumped the floor—the animal's happiness inside her too much for her dog's flesh to hide—but the way she looked Drake in the eye was with a particular intelligence that he had not seen in two decades. Drake's vision blurred and he pulled his sleeve across his eyes to clear it.

The terrier seemed to be assessing him and he felt suddenly self-conscious of his hipster haircut, tight black pants and melodramatic rings.

The dog barked as if unable to rein in her physical enthusiasm one second longer. Drake's father, wrapped inside this dog's body, leapt into his arms in a frenzy of canine affection.

Drake buried his face against the dog's warm, furry back. He thought, *Here is my father, in my arms, finally, he's come back*, and Drake held on, his face hot, his hands shaking.

"Should I take my leave of you, Grand Magician?" Adam knelt on one knee beside him, setting his guitar case on the floor. He must have gone back to get it from the patio. Adam gazed at the dog for a moment before a look of terrifying recognition broke across his face and he addressed Drake's father directly. "Say, don't you live in the South Court? You've lost your collar, haven't you?"

Drake's father hid his face in Drake's chest and let out a thin whine. The dog's small body trembled.

"Yes," Drake found himself saying though it felt as if the admission had been yanked out of his throat rather than simply spoken. "She belongs to Lord Roscoe."

Drake didn't know who had removed the dog's restraining collar, but he could take an easy guess. Magical law required Drake to return the dog to her master. Noncompliance would mean giving up his own soul to the king.

Drake cursed Everett—not an actual curse, merely a vicious wish for nonfatal harm to befall him soon—for forcing him to decide whether or not to return his father to that humiliating existence. The decision should have been easy. He should have been a good son and risked everything, regardless of the cost. Yet the terrier before him was the most eloquent and convincing argument imaginable for why he did not want to lose his soul.

Would he be caught? Certainly. Here stood Adam Wexley, the most innocent of bystanders, witnessing that Lord Roscoe's terrier had been seen in Drake's company. A crack team of sleuths would not be necessary to uncover his crime; average policemen following routine procedure would do.

Drake thought of killing Adam right then and eliminating the witness. But he knew he could never kill Adam. Drake's father had made and lost a drunken, thoughtless wager that subsequently destroyed his family. That wasn't Adam's fault.

"She's quite an elderly girl, isn't she?" Adam reached out to touch the terrier, who growled and snapped at his fingers. He frowned, apparently hurt by the terrier's spontaneous aggression. "We've always been friends until now. She sits with me sometimes when Lord Roscoe's entourage comes to visit the West Court."

Drake stood, still holding his father in his arms. His legs felt weak and sickness surged through him, as though every part of his body was somehow made capable of wanting to vomit. "Is your driver waiting for you?"

"I came by taxi," Adam said.

"Maybe we should share a taxi to the palace." Drake's heart felt like it was being ground down into paste. "So I can take this dog back home."

While Adam gathered his guitar and case, Drake found his shoes and keys while keeping the dog firmly in his grip. The silent elevator ride, though only thirteen floors long, seemed eternal. Downstairs he hailed a taxi and they sat in the backseat, not touching.

Drake held the dog on his lap without looking at her, able only occasionally to mumble the words "I'm sorry" while the terrier pawed at his chest and whined.

Outside the taxi window, Drake watched the high rose-marble wall of the outer palace wall slide by. Up ahead a soulless crew cleaned graffiti and mud. One tall, lanky gray-haired man stood out. The terrier leapt to the window and barked furiously. The soulless man looked up at the barking dog and at Drake, without recognition.

It was too much.

"Stop!" Drake seized the taxi driver's shoulder. "Stop here!"

The driver swerved into the loading zone and pulled the car to a halt. Their eyes met via the rearview mirror and the driver averted his gaze, waiting for Drake's next order. Drake turned to Adam. "How would you like to earn a boon? Any boon you'd like?"

"I would," Adam said eagerly, then shrank back from Drake's hard, searching gaze. "But what would I have to do?"

"I want you to forget you saw this dog."

Adam's eyes narrowed. "What are you going to do to her?"

"No harm will come to her, I swear to you on the Sea of Stars." Drake tried to keep his voice as calm and assured as possible, because now that he'd committed to the course of freeing his father, the clock was ticking. The moment Lord Roscoe realized the terrier was missing, he would call Drake's father's soul back, leaving him holding an empty, contraband dog. "I want her for my own and I want to release you from the burden of knowing about it."

"I don't want my memory erased." Adam's voice did not betray the fear Drake could see growing in his face. Drake sensed that Adam was just astute enough to know that a magician could, and would, take his memory whether he consented or not. "I don't want to be one of those people who don't know where they've been all night and always wonder what happened to them."

"You won't be. I won't leave a black hole in your memory for you to fill up with imaginary horror. Only the worst magicians have to resort to that artless butchery."

"What will happen then?"

"I will simply move your awareness of this dog from being something you actually encountered today to something you might have seen somewhere at sometime. That's all."

Adam spent a moment considering Drake's statement. That moment, for Drake and for his father, lasted ages. Finally, Adam said, "I suppose that it is polite of you to not make me an accomplice in your dognapping."

"Just so," Drake replied. The terrier walked across the seat and laid its paw on Adam's thigh. Adam tentatively reached out to pet her. The terrier accepted Adam's affection, leaning into his palm.

"She does seem to like you," Adam said, smiling.

"And I like her," Drake replied. "She wants to be with me."

"Is she your enchanted lover?" Adam blurted out.

The dog let out a horrified yelp of denial and squeezed her eyes shut, shaking her head as if she could physically fling the suggestion out of her brain. Drake merely repressed a shudder. "The less you know, the less I have to make you unlearn."

"Yes, of course." Adam's face crinkled up in grudging acceptance of this logic. "And what will my boon be?"

"Whatever you'd like, within the bounds of my power and excluding possession of my soul. I'm saving that for a rainy day."

Adam nodded resolutely. "I want to know where Lord Sapphire will be tonight."

This was the first time Drake had ever heard Adam speak of Lord Sapphire and the first time he ever felt that serpentine curl of envy around his heart.

"Is that really all you want? It's too little to ask in exchange for your memory," Drake said. His father spun around and eyed him as if he was crazy to argue. Drake ignored him. "I can give you far greater boons. Powers. Riches. I can deliver you your enemies locked inside the bodies of tiny, ugly parakeets."

He glanced up into the rearview mirror again and noted the taxi driver's obvious agreement.

"I have no enemies," Adam said.

"Very well." Drake raised his hand and whispered a charm over his spider ring causing her long metal legs to twitch and stretch. When he put his hand on Adam's shoulder, Adam flinched.

"Stay still."

Spider detached herself from the band, walked off Drake's hand, climbed up the side of Adam's neck then scampered across his cheek. She came to rest with her legs straddling Adam's right eye. She turned her head to look down into Adam's pupil.

"Don't blink." He spoke coldly, like he always did when he concentrated. A tiny beam of red light shone out of the spider's eyes. Adam's iris contracted reflexively.

"Will she bite me?"

"No." Drake looked through Adam's pupil into his thoughts. Adam was desperately afraid of what was happening, but determined that Drake should not know. Universally, people who were about to submit themselves to magic felt fear. So much so that Drake had come to consider terror in his subjects to be passé and rather disdain them for it. Not with Adam, though. He felt an uncharacteristic desire to reassure. "It's all right, I won't hurt you. I won't work any magics beyond our agreement. Now, think of this Lord Sapphire."

Adam relaxed into Drake's thrall and obediently visualized the moping courtier of his recent fantasies. Drake saw Lord

Thomas Myrdin of the South Court lying, in glorious lassitude, next to a pond popular with the suicidally morose.

Lord Myrdin was not in Drake's direct acquaintance, but he was well known in all four courts for his persistent proximity to King Louis. Sometimes the two of them would spend entire weekends together, such was their great friendship. Many said the king's kindness sprang from guilt over the execution of young Myrdin's parents when the boy was just eleven years old. Drake personally harbored no fantasies about the selfless motivation of the king or anyone else in the four courts.

Drake had never liked Myrdin. He seemed weak. He liked him less knowing that Adam admired him. But a deal was a deal. Drake checked the position of the stars in the sky.

"Remember that Lord Sapphire is in the Garden of the Winter Moon," Drake said. Then it was easy for him to reach into Adam's memory and pluck apart the connections linking himself with Lord Roscoe's terrier. Once they were removed from each other and from any sense of importance, Adam's own mind would do the work of erasing the irrelevant information in a couple of days. Drake whispered another word and Spider returned to him.

Drake woke Adam with a snap of his fingers. "We're here. Thank you very much for tonight."

"It was my pleasure. I only wish I could have stayed longer but I have another engagement." He turned to the taxi driver. "What do I owe?"

"Allow me," Drake offered, before the terrified taxi driver could formulate a response. Adam disappeared into the palace without a single look back. Drake tried not to be disappointed. Instead, he turned his attention to the taxi driver who had been monitoring the procedure, via the rearview mirror. Sweat trickled down his temple as Drake smiled at him.

"And how would you like to earn a boon for yourself?" Drake asked.

His brown eyes widened in a mix of terror and excitement. "I would like that very much, sir."

"Then help me get that man"—Drake pointed to the soulless custodian on the sidewalk—"into this cab."

Chapter Four

Adam raced across the palace grounds, breathless and hopeful, leaping over low sculptures and dodging small, treacherous fountains. He had suddenly gotten the idea that Lord Sapphire might be found in the Garden of the Winter Moon and could not wait to find out if he was right. He'd deduced this while at Grand Magician Drake's condo.

His reasoning went as follows: If Lord Sapphire was fond of Rexellan songs, then he might also enjoy spending time in the places that the songs mentioned. Many buildings in the palace grounds had been renovated over time. Some had even been razed and replaced with new modern structures. Of the ancient buildings, only the Garden of the Winter Moon had been commissioned by Queen Rexella herself. If Lord Sapphire were to be found anywhere, it would be there.

And he was right! Lord Sapphire lay on a stone bench staring up at the night sky with an expression of exquisite sorrow. His formal robes lay open at the chest and drooped over the edges of the bench as artistically as if they'd been carved there. Adam thought he looked more like a sculpture than a man. His hand lay across his bare chest.

Adam drew near. Lord Sapphire did not notice him.

"Do you mind if I sit here?" he asked.

Lord Sapphire roused himself and caught sight of Adam.

"Suit yourself."

Adam followed Lord Sapphire's gaze up into the night sky, remembering what Drake had said about a new star. He wondered which one it was. Not being a great observer of the heavens, Adam recognized only two constellations and neither of them had gained an interloper. He wished that he'd asked Drake when he had the chance, so he could point it out to Lord Sapphire. Instead he asked, "Observing the stars?"

"I'm waiting for something," Lord Sapphire replied.

"Is it me?"

"If you like." Lord Sapphire drew a hand across his face and Adam saw no ring on his finger.

"You're not wearing your sapphire."

"My ring, you mean?" Lord Sapphire coughed out a short, bitter laugh and made a bloodless gesture toward the pool. "I threw it in there."

"But it was so beautiful!" Adam rushed to the edge of the pool. The moonlight was bright and his eyes were sharp. The gold and pink ring sparkled on the pool's white marble bottom. "Look, it's right there."

"You're welcome to it."

"You'll want it again, I'm sure." Adam had once thrown his favorite toy car into a lake in a fit of childish rage and imagined that Lord Sapphire had acted in much the same mood. He waded into the fountain, soaking himself to the knees. He picked it up and held it out to Lord Sapphire, who ignored him. He moved forward, knelt and slid the ring back on Lord Sapphire's chilly finger.

"Is this supposed to prove something?" His quiet question fell like lead into the soft summer night.

Adam drew back from Lord Sapphire, confused by the sliver of contempt in his expression. He sat on the marble edge of the moon pool, regarding Lord Sapphire with earnest concern. Adam said, "It's a beautiful ring," as if that explained everything.

"This ring is nothing but a piece of pretty rock set into a band of shiny metal. It's of value to a pawnbroker, maybe, but it means nothing to me."

"It must mean something or why would you throw it away?" Adam reasoned, thinking that because Lord Sapphire was speaking to him, he must be making positive progress.

"You're right. That is exactly why I threw it away in the first place." Lord Sapphire wrenched the ring off his finger and hurled it back into the fountain. "Leave it for some other unlucky man to find. At least then I won't be alone in hell."

"You're not alone." Adam spoke out of reflex.

"Because you're with me, I suppose?" Lord Sapphire smiled a deep, sarcastic smile. "Will your music work the magic that will ease my troubled heart?"

"It could if you wanted it to," Adam said and he believed it. Lord Sapphire seemed, for a moment to fill with rage, then detachment smoothed over his features once again.

"I don't want to be mended," Lord Sapphire said tiredly. "But you can play me a song anyway if you like."

Eager to comply, Adam got out his guitar, only then remembering he'd broken a string. He thought that it wouldn't matter. He started to play the song he knew would please Lord Sapphire, changing it slightly as he had with Drake to accommodate the different fingering. Lord Sapphire laid a hand across his forehead appearing to suffer a small twinge of pain each time Adam had to modify the song. He found himself unwillingly comparing Lord Sapphire to Drake. It was unwilling because Adam had supposed that any comparison between the two of them would be weighted in Lord Sapphire's favor, and yet here he was thinking Drake a more attentive and appreciative audience than the object of his crush.

And Lord Sapphire wasn't even listening. He stared at his watch as if counting each passing second. Adam played two more songs before, to his relief, Lord Sapphire sat up.

"Much as I appreciate your playing, Lord Wexley, I fear I have business to attend to in the royal residence."

"Please let me walk with you."

"Only if you promise to leave me if I command it." Lord Sapphire seemed very intent and Adam nodded earnestly.

"Certainly, I will."

"Then come." Lord Sapphire led Adam out of the Garden of the Winter Moon, but rather than taking the flagged pathway that marked the route between the royal residence and the South Court, he walked straight in and took a turn toward the east.

Adam balked, having no desire to get lost in the labyrinth this late at night. "Are you sure this is the way?"

Lord Sapphire smiled. "It's a short cut. Are you worried you'll get lost?"

"Of course. I've no idea how to get around outside the flagged routes. I'm lost every time I try."

"I know every turn and corner of this labyrinth." For the first time that evening, Lord Sapphire's expression gentled. "I've walked this maze for years and years. I won't let you get lost." Lord Sapphire took Adam's hand, pulling him gently through the turns and switchbacks, moving with assurance and ease.

"Do you really know which direction we're going?"

"Right now, north. Once we turn that corner, east, then an immediate turn left will take us to the labyrinth's center and the royal residence." Lord Sapphire smiled back at him.

"How long did it take you to learn this?" Adam couldn't imagine how many times a person would have to tread the same twisting path in order to completely memorize it.

"I've been living at the South Court for eighteen years," Lord Sapphire said. "But I learned the maze during the first ten or so. It's like learning court manners. It just happens over time without your noticing."

Two turns later they stood at the entrance in the clearing in front of the royal residence. Lord Sapphire again checked his watch. "You know, I think I might want my ring after all."

"Do you? Shall I go fetch it for you?"

"Would you be so kind? I have an appointment here that I cannot miss."

"I'll go right away." Adam turned and faced the entrance to the labyrinth, but hesitated. "I don't think I remember the way we came."

"You shouldn't go in there if you're uncertain," Lord Sapphire said. "Use the flagged route. At least you'll know where you are."

"Where shall I meet you to return your ring?"

"I'm sure you'll be able to find me. I trust you to keep it until then."

Adam took his leave and walked jauntily down the road leading back to South Court, happy to have received the clear invitation to see Lord Sapphire again and eager to find the ring that was his ticket.

Everett's house lay at the edge of the city where the suburbs dissipated into terraced farmland. His estate house was small by noble standards, only two stories of carved marble façade on a measly ten acres of land. The interior had been updated with modern amenities like electricity and plumbing, but the rooms were otherwise the same as they had been for the last three hundred or so years. The sole modern architectural additions to the property were two big glass aviaries arched off either side of his house like glittering wings. As a hobby he bred inhabitable birds. Drake's mother had always said that the sound of their fluttering wings reminded her of Paradise while the stink of their crap conjured up pictures of Hell, proving the perfect ethical balance of nature.

Although this estate had never been home, Drake had often visited while his mother had lived here, so he knew the property well and the servants knew him. The gateman waved the taxi through immediately without even calling ahead to the main house. They parked in the circle drive, and Drake let the terrier and his father's soulless body get out and stretch their legs while he attended to the cabby's amnesia, paid him and sent him on his way.

The terrier caught sight of the birds in the aviary and she was away, racing up and down the length of the aviary, barking. This attracted the attention of Everett's butler, a human servant who stood in the open doorway with a blasé expression that said that he'd expected Drake's arrival. Drake's father's soulless body stood sullenly on Everett's lawn shifting from foot to foot, uneasily.

"I'm not supposed to leave work," he mumbled. "I'm going to get in trouble."

He'd been saying much the same thing the entire ride out to Everett's and each time Drake had quieted him the same way. He pulled a bag of salt-water taffy out of his satchel and held out a piece to his father. Numb, but still desirous, his father reached out for the candy. Drake held it away, edging slowly toward the front door of the house.

"I'll give it to you once we get inside," Drake coaxed him. "Come on now." The terrier raced around them as they crossed the vast green lawn and entered the gilded front doors. As the door shut behind them, Drake looked down at the terrier.

"Do you think there's ever been a lottery that wasn't fixed by some magician or other?" he asked. The dog shook her head no.

Thinking himself unobserved, Drake's father made a grab for the candy, then submissively recoiled when Drake noticed and rebuked him.

"I'm going to get in trouble." His mumble became a whine.

"You'll be all right." Drake unwrapped the taffy and gave it to his father's body. The old man jammed it into his mouth greedily and closed his eyes as he chewed it, delighted as a toddler. He loved taffy and his tongue remembered that it was his favorite, even though his mind did not. When Drake was a child, it was always his birthday gift to his father, and he felt as though he was replaying a scene from his single-digit years feeding it to him again. Only with one difference, when he'd possessed his soul, Drake hadn't been required to unwrap the candy to prevent his father from ingesting the waxed paper.

A large, green parrot flew down to land on the side table standing in Everett's black and white foyer. The terrier was unable to resist another round of fierce barking. Startled, the parrot flew upward to rest on a higher sconce.

Father's soulless body watched the bird. He said, "Pretty..." through a mouthful of taffy.

"Master Everett is not at home," the parrot squawked. "Can I show you to a room, Grand Magician?"

"Yes, and I'll need to have a change of clothes sent up after me."

"Very good, sir."

Once up the stairs, his father's body didn't want to enter the guest room. He held his sinewy arms straight against the doorframe, shaking his head, eyes pressed closed. The terrier seized hold of his pant leg and yanked with all the force of her small body, but his father's body didn't budge.

"I'm not allowed inside bedrooms," he moaned. "I'll get in trouble."

"It will be all right," Drake cooed, trying to gently pry his father's fingers off the wall. "If you go inside I'll give you more candy."

"No!" the body shouted. "No! No! No! You're bad!"

The terrier let go of his pant leg and jumped up on the bed barking furiously at Drake. Although he didn't understand the language of animals, the terrier's message was clear: *We don't have much time! Do something.*

Drake stepped back and rammed his father's body, sending it flying into the room. His father's body stumbled down to the floor and immediately tried to scramble back out. Drake closed and locked the door. He turned, expecting to see the old man cowering on the silk carpet, but even soulless, Drake's father was intractable. He slammed his body into Drake, fumbling for the doorknob, face convulsed in moronic hysteria.

"I have to go back to work!" Spittle flew from his lips with each syllable. "You are not my master! I'm telling!"

Drake grabbed his father's arms, trying to kick the older man's feet out from under him.

The dog barked and bit Drake's father's calf. His father's body howled in pain, tears streaming down his face.

Drake normally didn't choose violence as a problem-solver. He had found that however satisfying it may be to kick a man to the ground, kneel on his chest and stab a paralyzing ring into his throat, there was usually a better way.

On this night, though, he didn't have time to search for that better way.

Drake stomped on his father's body's ankle and when he crumpled in pain, he drove a fast kick hard into the older man's abdomen. His father's body went down, hitting his head hard on the wooden floor. Blood spurted out from a cut on his scalp, and his sobs became convulsive and angry. He flailed his arms and legs in every direction like a toddler. Drake knelt on his chest and jabbed the end of his talon ring into the skin—not piercing the surface, just making contact.

The soul Drake kept inside this ring was black with lust for bondage. Drake had bought him at his execution, and stripped his soul down to his most singular desire. Now Drake let him out only when he needed to keep a person motionless. The soul obeyed Drake because tying people up was what Talon had liked to do best during his flesh life. Drake never let him go as far as he would like.

Black, oily stripes oozed out of Drake's ring as the bindings wrapped around his father's body. He lay still, eyes rolling in terror. He foamed and wailed. A black stripe seeped across his mouth, stifling his voice to low moans.

Drake got off him and turned to the terrier.

"Get up on the bed."

The terrier complied. It jumped up on the rumpled coverlet and then rolled over submissively onto its back. Her tail wagged but Drake could also see suspicion in her eyes. Animal panic. The dog's spirit instinctively feared this posture.

"Lie still." Drake held the dog's throat with one hand and raised the other to his lips. He whispered a spell over his blood diamond, then pressed the ring against his own throat. He exhaled, leaned down and fitted his mouth over the terrier's. He sucked hard, pulling his father's soul out of the dog's body and into his own lungs.

He did not exhale.

He rushed to his father's body and jabbed Talon into one of the black stripes and called his slave soul back into his cell. Before the body could begin to struggle or wail, he pressed his lips against the body's mouth, blowing the soul into its rightful flesh. As soon as he felt the weight of it slide from his mouth, he pulled away and clamped his hand over Father's lips to keep the spirit from sliding out.

Drake's father's eyes cleared and he blinked. He shoved Drake aside and sat up, coughing and spitting.

"What kind of soul transfer was that? Hell's Stars! In my day we'd have just cut the dog's head off and forced the body to drink its blood."

"My method requires less dry cleaning." Drake climbed to his feet and dragged the back of his hand across his mouth. He'd never relished the idea of mouth to mouth with a dog. Immediately replicating that action with the paterfamilias left him with the strong desire to brush his teeth. Fortunately, his suite had a bathroom. He excused himself and made for the cream-tiled room, seeking toothbrush and perhaps even mouthwash.

While Drake applied the toothpaste, he could hear his father talking to the terrier, calling her a good girl, whispering that they were both free now. Drake smiled. His father couldn't be seriously angry that Drake's methods had left the terrier alive.

Drake's servant, Nancy, had said much the same thing to the greyhound she'd shared a body with. He didn't relish having to tell his father they had to return the dog to Lord Roscoe.

He lingered in the bathroom, both nervous of facing his father and cursing his own bashfulness. He ran his hands through his hair, for the first time in his life trying to make it look plainer. What did he have to fear? He was the hero, breaking every law of magical ownership for his father, yet there he stood, hiding in the bathroom weighing whether or not his father would like his haircut.

Outside Drake heard his father saying, "Where's Zachary? Go find Zachary," in that special tone people use to incite excitement in dogs. The terrier yipped and scratched the bathroom door.

Drake brought back a towel from the bathroom and handed it to his father. "The back of your head's bleeding."

Now that his father was free from canine impulse, his characteristic reserve had returned. They did not embrace, as they had before. His father merely clapped him on the shoulder at arm's length. Drake remembered this gesture from countless boyhood encounters. It made him weak with nostalgia.

"You hit me hard enough, didn't you, Zachary?" His father placed the towel gingerly on the back of his skull then pulled it away to observe the level of bleeding. The spot of blood marring the towel's white plushness elicited only a snort of derision.

"Do you want me to heal the cut?"

"A tiny thing like this?" His father shook his head. "Don't waste your strength on that. You'll need it later."

While his words were undoubtedly true, something in his tone implied more specific foreknowledge.

"To hide you?" Drake asked.

"Hide me? God, no! I don't need any help from you to hide. It may have been twenty years, but I still have some very valuable knowledge. Any number of magicians would take me in." His laugh was short and bitter, and it stung Drake.

"What then?"

"Clifton's going to activate the East Court medallion tonight to cover my escape. But he needs my camp-knife locus to do it. I'm praying to the Sea of Stars that you still have it." His father caught sight of himself in the mirror and drew forward, horror and revulsion playing across his face as he saw his body for the first time in years.

"Of course I do. Mother gave me all your things."

"You need to get it to Clifton. He can't break through the barrier of protective spells without it. Listen, though. The camp knife has four blades, one for each of the medallions. Make sure he uses the correct blade." His father tried to smooth his wild, wiry hair into place, but it only sprang back up in tufts.

"How can I tell which blade is which?"

"They're labeled." His tone conveyed how obvious he felt the answer to Drake's question was. "I don't want him to bungle a magical action that powerful. The backlash could kill him."

"What reason is Everett going to give for using the medallion?" The Medallion of Amabel, guarded by the East Court held within it the power of the Severing Wind, which could cut through the bond between body and soul.

"If all goes well, he won't need to provide a reason. Clifton has it on high authority that there will be an attempt to assassinate the princess tonight. It should be easy to transfer blame for both crimes onto the poor wretch. And the Severing Wind should knock enough souls out of their flesh that no one will investigate too closely. You won't be suspected."

"What will happen to the other souls?" Drake did not try to conceal how much this plan disturbed him.

His father smiled in an unkind fashion that Drake had never seen before. "Don't worry. They won't go to waste. Lord Roscoe's soul especially will not go to waste."

Drake felt cold and ill at the thought of so many people being severed from their bodies, with no hope of return. That his father didn't care about this shouldn't have surprised him. It was what magicians did, how they worked. The fate of the unfortunate souls who fueled their magic was of no consequence, and while Drake would have recriminated anyone else for their callousness, he could not be unhappy his father was free and no one would suspect Drake of aiding his release.

His father clapped a hand on his shoulder again, perhaps sensing his reluctance and withdrawal. "You'd best get moving, Zachary."

"Back to the palace? Already?" Drake wasn't ready to leave his father yet. He'd only just reinstalled him in his flesh. They'd barely had a chance to speak.

His father apparently understood this and gripped his shoulder more tightly. "I know, I wish we had more time too. But we will. Once I get established I'll call for you."

"Will you tell me where you're going?"

His father shook his head. "It's better if you know nothing if the King's Police come."

"I'm an excellent liar." Drake tried to get the old man to relent. If he must leave now, so be it. But he needed a better assurance that they would meet soon.

"I'm sure you are. But it's easier if you don't have to." He smirked and Drake could see himself in that expression. He saw himself telling Adam it was better that he knew nothing.

"What if I need to contact you?"

"Don't be difficult, Zachary." His father suddenly looked gray and tired as if it took massive strength to keep his tenuous connection to his own flesh. Sweat trickled down his forehead.

"Are you all right?"

"Yes, of course. Go on now. Everett's servants will take care of me." He squeezed Drake's shoulder then said, as an afterthought, "Take the dog with you. She wants to get back to her marrow bone."

As his father turned away, Drake tossed a tiny spell onto his back, a marker, that would help him find his father. He egressed from Everett's estate, as he had been bidden.

Chapter Five

For Myrdin, gaining entrance to the palace posed no obstacle. Familiar guards let him walk up the wide malachite-tiled stairs and through the vast doors without questioning him. Only when he ascended the stairs and tried to enter the princess's nursery, did any guard impede his progress. Two of them. Humans. Outside the door.

Myrdin smiled at them as they crossed their lances in front of him.

"I have a gift to bring the princess. Please let me pass."

"No one enters without King Louis or Lady Carolyn's permission." The guard, a redhead who Myrdin remembered from previous visits to Louis's chambers, looked sheepish. "I'm sorry, my lord."

"Surely an exception can be made for me." Myrdin reached for the door handle. The guard shoved him back and let out a shrill whistle. Myrdin slammed into the opposite wall. The nursery door opened. Four more guards rushed out. Lance points descended, all pointing at him. Myrdin smiled again. He felt the light inside him surge, dulling his emotions but sharpening his senses.

"I mean no harm." He turned his right hand over, revealing the painting of the butterfly. "As you can see, I'm unarmed."

As he spoke he pressed some of the star's light through his hand. A transparent red butterfly flew up from his palm, fluttering before the guards, who stood transfixed. Some stared with desire, others suspicion, depending on their temperaments, but none could look away. The butterfly flew in big, lazy circles down the hallway. One guard jabbed at it with his lance. Another shoved the weapon aside, saying, "Don't hurt it."

The nursery door hung open. Myrdin stood, walked in and closed the door behind him. The child slept in a green, canopied cradle in the center of the room. A chimpanzee nanny wearing a collar of West Court gold dozed in a rocking chair nearby. All around the two of them, a thick wall of spells had been drawn. Myrdin knelt on one knee and removed his paintbrush from its case. He focused the light through its tip, drawing a door in the air before him, a way in through the spells. Once finished, he pushed the door open. The princess's defensive spells recoiled from him, not breaking, simply moving aside to let him pass.

Elation filled him.

His magic, the light from his star, easily overpowered these spells set by the most powerful magicians of the Royal Academy of Magic. He would prove himself tonight. Fate had chosen him. As he drew near, the nanny woke with a start. Myrdin revealed his other palm, the petals of the drawn peony flew out of it, swirling in a cloud around the nanny who stared in wonder then leapt after them, trying to catch them. He lifted the baby and, holding her with one arm, fished through his pocket for the watch.

He had the watch in his hand. He'd gained entrance thirteen minutes too early. Everett would not be ready yet. He had to wait. He looked into the baby's face.

She looked at him and his heart clenched with remorse. Was he really the kind of man who could kill an infant? He sat back in the rocking chair. This would hurt Louis so much. When he'd been deep in nightmares, this act had seemed inevitable. The baby kicked, her face convulsed and it looked like she might cry. Myrdin quickly wrote the word *sleep* on her forehead and soon she yawned. Her eyes drooped shut.

Myrdin took a deep breath, focused on the light inside him. This baby would unleash destruction. Kill thousands. It had to be done.

Drake arrived at the entrance to the South Court breathless and holding a squirming terrier. He released the dog and she scampered off through the South Court garden, barking. Drake entered the labyrinth and turned down the flagged path between the South and East Courts, constantly quickening his pace until he was running, the muggy summer air thick as sludge in his lungs. Clouds of gnats hung in the air in the narrow corridors between high, mazelike hedges. Here and there the labyrinth opened into a clearing, with a small fountain or fish pool ringed by stone benches. Courtiers lounged there, trysting or scheming. No one paid Drake any attention.

A fashionable man rushing through the summer night was no unusual sight for them.

He reached the East Court gate and stepped through the great carved arch. He nodded to a courtier, a woman dressed in East Court colors, who sat smoking a hooka. The woman nodded back, stroking the thick neck of a docile tiger that lounged beside her. Inhabited, of course. Minutes from now that tiger would have free will. Drake felt somewhat responsible for the mauling that would likely ensue.

The idea gave him pause, but it had to be done. For his father and for himself. Drake took a few steps past them, hoping that the tiger would retain some affection for the woman once its soul was gone, then against his better judgment, turned back.

"Getting a little late to be outside, isn't it?"

"Donald likes to be outside at night." The woman indicated the tiger next to her.

"Look, do you see that star?" Drake pointed up at the Ghost Star.

The woman turned her pale blue eyes upward.

"That star is very bad luck for enchanted creatures. They shouldn't be out while it is shining."

"According to whom?" the woman asked.

"The Royal Academy of Magic." Drake held up his blood diamond to show her the academy emblem decorating the band. Donald cocked his head, regarding the ring and Drake with that cutting intelligence that he found unnerving in larger inhabited animals. Then Donald pushed himself up to his big paws and started padding off into East Court. The woman gathered up her hookah and set out after him.

"Drake, you remain incorrigibly good."

Turning back toward the gate, Drake spotted Everett. The older man stood, hands jammed into the pockets of his rumpled suit, smug grin on his face.

"It's not goodness so much as a lack of ambivalence toward the fate of others," Drake replied.

"Even total strangers?"

"Almost everyone's a total stranger to me."

"Fair enough." Everett drew close. "How is he?"

Drake didn't have to ask of whom Everett spoke.

"Back to his old self again."

Everett nodded, his smile deepening and growing tender. "That's good news."

"I left him at your house." Drake opened his palm to reveal the edge of his father's slim red camping knife. "He sent me with this. The blades are labeled, one for each medallion."

Everett covered Drake's palm with his. For one second he hesitated, not wanting to be demoted to his childhood function, running messages and tools between Everett and Father. He felt like he'd been pushed backward two decades toward naïve youth. Everett obviously felt Drake's hesitation but mistook his motive for ethical reserve.

"It has to be done." He gently pulled the knife from Drake's hand. "Or we'll all three lose our souls. I know you like to command the moral high ground, but sometimes it isn't so simple."

"I never said it was." Drake let go of the knife.

"You should get clear." Everett tapped Drake's talon ring. "You wouldn't want them getting loose."

"It would take more than a broken medallion to unbind my rings." Drake spoke without egotism. No soul, no magician, no spell had ever been able to undo his hold on a soul that he owned.

"I still don't think you need to test it by being too close," Everett cautioned. Drake withdrew, leaving Everett to commit high treason in peace. He went quickly, retracing his previous steps through the maze, cursing every unnecessary turn. What a royal conceit, this labyrinth. Forcing everyone to follow a preplanned and disorienting path in order to meet each other, or see the sovereign.

It wasn't as if the labyrinth provided an impenetrable defense. They were only bushes, after all. Annoying bushes.

Drake had just reached the South Court gate when he saw Adam, sauntering along, terrier in his arms. He scratched the dog behind her ears.

Of course he would be here out in the open at the worst possible time, Drake thought. *He could not be a sensible person, locked away in his room behind a nice solid door.*

Drake decided then to force Adam to come home with him. It was what he wanted to do anyway. Parting company with his father had reopened an old and lonely ache that he longed to soothe with the flesh of another man.

"Lord Wexley!" Drake called. Adam turned to the sound of Drake's voice and in a moment recognized him. Not with pleasure or disgust, but with an acceptance that told Drake that Adam had expected to see him again.

The air around Drake tensed with dense pressure, as if he'd dived into the deep ocean. The feeling of massively wrought spells being undone, the feeling of Everett cracking open the power of the Medallion of Amabel. There was no time even to run. Adam looked to the sky, sensing the change without seeing it. The terrier struggled out of his arms and went tearing into the South Court gate.

"The medallion has cracked!" Drake shouted. "Get down!"

"The what?"

"The Medallion of Amabel—" Drake began, but was cut off when red lightning crackled across the sky. He tackled Adam, pulling him to the ground just as the blast of spectral wind hit them like a wall. Adam coughed and half his soul flew out of his mouth before Drake grasped it and pressed it back in. Out of some reflex, Adam wrapped his arms around Drake, cradling Drake's head against his chest, apparently to protect him. Drake kept his hand pressed against Adam's mouth as the wind and lightning surged over them, as the raw power of it cracked fissures in the bonds holding all souls in place.

Drake's rings vibrated as the bound spirits inside sensed their chance at freedom. But their silver prisons held fast until the Severing Wind subsided and they were once again powerless in servitude.

Then the noise and the violence stopped.

Drake lay awkwardly atop Adam with his hand pressed over Adam's mouth. Adam kept his arms wrapped around Drake, as if waiting for a second round of calamity. The courtyard silence was broken suddenly by the sound of feline roars, dog barks and avian cries as the dozens of inhabited animals of the court found themselves abruptly alone inside their bodies. Cautiously, Drake pulled his hand from Adam's mouth.

"What happened?"

"The inhabited animals are free," Drake shouted above the simian cacophony currently erupting from the West Court. "We have to get out of here."

"Free?" Adam shoved Drake off his chest. "I must go to the princess."

"Princess?" Drake rolled to his feet. "You mean the baby?"

"Her nanny is a chimpanzee." Adam was already running and Drake, feeling a fool, ran after him.

"Adam, she'll be all right!"

If Adam heard, he made no response. Clear loyalty drew him toward the royal residence. He ran toward the princess, his expression fearless and single-minded. Earsplitting claxons pounded the night. Apes of every description rushed and cavorted through the labyrinth, alternately chasing and being chased by servants. Two orangutans sat busily dismantling a limousine that had crashed into a shallow fountain. Drake caught Adam's arm and tried to explain that the baby had other protectors and that, even uninhabited, a chimpanzee would not likely harm the precious little darling.

"You can't be sure of that." Adam pulled his arm away, his voice resonated with a singular devoted purpose. That devotion made Drake jealously wish that Adam searched this open-air zoo for Drake's sake. But Drake didn't need rescuing so Adam did not look at him. And Drake was forced to trail behind him like a dog.

But at least I am a dog with useful skills. Even though Drake did not dare loose the souls in his rings, he could still conjure an image of the baby in a pool of water left from the cracked and gushing fountain.

"Look." Drake pulled Adam down to one knee beside him. The image of the baby girl, swathed in her green silk blanket shimmered across the water's surface. She was being held against the shoulder of a man in fine red robes. A thick gold watch chain was wound three times around the princess's neck. The other end of the chain was tied around the man's slashed wrist. Blood slowly traveled along the chain, moving against all common understanding of physics.

Drake had seen the man before and the image of him did not fit with the baby. He also did not like the look of that watch chain. Everett's locus. No wonder he needed a different tool to crack the Medallion of Amabel. His own locus was being used by Thomas Myrdin. But even that seemed wrong. Did Myrdin really know enough magic to be performing this spell? Drake focused power through his blood diamond. Images slid across the surface of the water, misty and gyrating. They coalesced into the shape of the nursery. Myrdin held the shrieking baby against his own shoulder, speaking, his face terrible with hurt and hatred. Guards crowded the doors but didn't dare come close.

"Sapphire?" Adam reached out to touch Myrdin's face and disrupted the image. His confusion seemed total. "What's going on?"

"I'm not sure." One thing he did know was that Everett's pocket watch in Thomas Myrdin's hands meant the night would get worse.

"Come on!" Adam raced down one narrow garden path toward the royal residence and Drake followed, cursing when they both came up short at a dead end. Broken branches and debris littered the ground. Limp, breathing, vacant human bodies lay everywhere while animals roamed free.

Drake shook his head in disgust. "This is absurd."

"We missed the flagged route." Adam started to turn back but Drake caught him.

"We're not taking that route." Drake raised his hand. He focused his rage through his blood diamond then sent it bursting concussively outward. The tall hedges of the labyrinth blasted apart, leaving a clear path to the center of the maze. Adam ran, Drake close behind him.

They burst into the open directly beside the statue of Queen Rexella mounted on its massive pedestal. Beneath her green patina visage, seven keepers who'd managed to keep their souls in their bodies fought a roaring bear that had not. Above, white hawks circled and attacked anything that ran beneath. More of Everett's familiars, no doubt. Screams split the night while echoing flashes of red lightning spread its fingers across the sky. Had Everett used the medallion again? How many times would he do it? Another gust of wind tore over the garden, sending pine needles and dirt sailing through the air. Drake reached for Adam, pulling him close against the base of a statue. Adam held on to Drake, teeth clenched together, face buried in Drake's shoulder, swallowing his soul back into himself until the wind subsided again. Caught in the wind's full force, the keepers lay motionless on the ground, while the bear pawed their inert forms.

All for my father, Drake felt so sick inside. *All for him.*

They ran for the palace. A thick line of guards stood directly inside the dome of shielding spells. They parted at the sight of Drake.

"Grand Magician! The princess—" one sputtered. Drake held up a silencing hand.

"Take us there!"

Chapter Six

The princess's room lay up a wide staircase now littered with the newly slain corpses of previously inhabited predators. Following Drake's lead, Adam stepped around a panther, over a wolf, and sidestepped two lions, one still breathing.

Guards lined the hallway. Adam kept close behind Drake, the image of Lord Sapphire's blood winding along the watch chain fresh in his mind, playing like a film loop. As they approached the open doorway, the king's voice floated out.

"My daughter has nothing to do with you and I, Thomas. She's just a baby."

"Do you think I'm doing this for revenge?" Lord Sapphire's voice took on a tremulous edge. "I told you. She will open the demon realm. She must die tonight. I'm sorry."

Adam's heart hardened against Lord Sapphire. He must have planned this all along. Sending Adam back to get his ring had been nothing but a way to ditch Adam so he could continue with his plan.

"No!" Adam pushed past Drake into the room without thinking, without hesitation. Lord Sapphire stood between the bassinet and an old rocking chair. His red formal robes cut a sharp contrast to the deep-green sheets of jade that tiled the walls. The gold chain stretching between him and the princess

Nicole Kimberling

was nearly completely red. Lord Sapphire's blood dripped out onto the floor.

Lord Sapphire caught sight of Adam and the rage on his face transformed to confusion and disbelief.

"I just can't shake you off, can I?" Lord Sapphire let out a short laugh. "Go back to the West Court, Lord Wexley. It's dangerous to be out tonight."

"I can't let you harm the princess." Adam straightened, shifting so that his guitar lay more comfortably against his back. "It is my duty."

"Your duty? Let me give you some advice, my young troubadour. Never do your duty. This is where doing your duty leads." Lord Sapphire started to pull the chain again and it tightened around the baby's neck. The princess let out a choking breath, but she did not cry, only gazed upward, held silent by some spell.

King Louis flinched but kept his distance.

Adam fell to his knees before Lord Sapphire, his hands clasped together, begging, "Please, spare the child."

"This spell cannot be undone." Lord Sapphire seemed moved by the honesty in Adam's voice and his grip on the baby slackened. "I'm sorry. I wish I had met you sooner."

"I've brought Grand Magician Drake. He can fix anything." Adam looked back. "Please, Grand Magician, help us."

Drake moved slowly into the room, hands up. Behind him soldiers leaned forward, readying themselves for attack. Drake glanced at the chain linking Lord Sapphire to the baby, but before he could speak the king's voice interrupted the silence.

"Yes," the king whispered from his place on the green velvet sofa. "Please, Thomas. Let this fellow take her. We can forget all this."

The soothing voice reignited Lord Sapphire's rage.

"You think I'm a mental case, don't you, Louis?" A scornful sneer ricked his face. "Maybe I am, but I can still save you."

He pulled the chain and convulsed, as though he was choking, then fell to the malachite-tiled floor still holding the princess in his arms. Red light spread out around them. Adam lunged forward desperate to retrieve the little girl but Drake caught his shoulder and yanked him backward.

"Don't. The spell is set in motion. Stopping it could kill them both."

Adam scrambled to his feet, but stayed right on the perimeter of the crimson light, his chest pressed against Drake's hand. Looking at Sapphire and the princess, Adam could have mistaken them for father and daughter, the way he held the little girl. King Louis recoiled back to the couch, the pain of ineffectuality etched into his face.

"Please, Grand Magician." Adam leaned close to Drake. "Do something."

"I will," Drake whispered, "when the time is right. We have to let the transfer happen."

"Transfer?" the king demanded. "Transfer of what?"

"I don't know yet," Drake replied coolly as he watched the chain intently. "It could be— Wait! There!"

The chain glowed brighter and brighter red, like an ember or a fiberoptic cable. The change was first noticeable in the princess, her baby fat melting away and her limbs lengthening. Lord Sapphire showed no change for at least a minute while the princess grew and grew. Then suddenly Adam could see that Lord Sapphire's face seemed younger, smoother.

"The transfer is age?" Adam's brow crinkled in consternation and he stopped pressing so strongly against Drake's restraining hand.

"Exactly." His hands free, Drake crouched down next to the two of them, his face bathed in hot red light. He reached into his pocket and drew out a pair of chic sunglasses and put them on. Their mirrored surface turned instantly molten with reflected light. "I think I know what to cut, but I need Your Majesty's permission."

The king watched, stricken as his baby daughter grew to a young child to an adolescent. Her nipples softened and small budding breasts appeared. Her swaddling blanket far too small to cover her nakedness, she lay, with a face as blank as a soulless husk while Lord Sapphire shrank. His muscles diminished, his handsomeness softened to prettiness and his clothes engulfed him.

Adam remained where he stood, transfixed with horror. He'd never seen much real magic worked before and had no idea that such a thing could be done. How could the man he'd played music for less than an hour ago be trying to kill Princess Julianna?

Only Drake seemed to understand what was happening, so he looked to the grand magician for direction. In turn Drake sought the king's consent.

"May I have permission to intercede, Your Majesty?" Drake bowed slightly, as though he were addressing the king at some routine state function.

"Do it!" The king looked away.

Adam knelt down beside Drake with the idea that he could somehow help. Drake regarded him with a strangely compassionate expression.

"You take the princess. I'll take the boy."

Adam gathered the lanky, nude princess up in his arms while Drake pulled a switchblade with an inscribed ebony handle from his pocket. He whispered something Adam could not hear, sliced through the chain as though it were made of silk. Blood poured out onto the floor. Adam pushed his hand against the princess's throat, applying pressure to try to stop the bleeding, but still the blood came. It took him a moment to realize the blood didn't come from her, but the arm of the recently youthened Lord Sapphire. When Adam looked up again, a tight circle of soldiers surrounded him, their spears and pistols all aimed at the inert and boyish form of Lord Sapphire.

"He's still bleeding," Adam told Drake.

"Good," the king growled. "Let him bleed."

Drake deftly wound a knot in the chain, which stopped the blood flow. To Adam's amazement, he gathered Lord Sapphire's body into his lap. Drake gave the surrounding soldiers a warning appraisal, and Adam saw several of them flinch away from his scrutiny.

"I believe that the princess is unharmed, Your Majesty. Apart from her body's acceleration, of course." Drake pushed his sunglasses up atop his head. His hands were red with blood and left wet marks in his black hair.

The king looked at his daughter in her full nudity, and then the gawking soldiers. Suddenly, he ordered the men from the room, roaring out his frustration at their fleeing backs. He ripped a coverlet from the rocking chair and draped it across her body. Roused by the sensation, the girl blinked and opened her eyes. Then she began to cry, the deafening, inconsolable sobs of a frightened infant, powered by eighteen-year-old lungs. Adam rocked her flailing body, ducking her flying arms, trying to restrain her without accidentally touching her free, pendulous breasts.

"Send for her nurse!" the king bellowed.

Lord Sapphire, newly a boy, began to rouse. Drake shoved the tip of his talon ring into the boy's throat. Lord Sapphire stilled immediately, as if paralyzed.

"This one is useless—a husk," Drake said. "Drained by the spell."

"He can still hang." The king slammed his foot into Myrdin's back. Drake pulled the boy's body closer.

"If it pleases you, Your Majesty, I still have some use for this body, and the sliver of a soul remains within it. May I have him as payment for services rendered today?"

The king regarded Drake for an uncertain moment. Adam plainly read the king's desire for vengeance warring with his practical knowledge of grand magicians. Above all, he didn't want to owe Drake a debt. Everyone knew that.

"So be it." He waved the boy's body away. "Have the contract brought from the South Court and get this traitor out of my sight."

Drake smiled tightly. He bowed to the king and nodded, then slung the boy over his shoulder and quit the palace, leaving Adam to wrangle the princess's infantile tantrum until a nurse who'd been unharmed by the magical events of the evening could be found. By then two hours had passed. The red lightning that had broken the night sky had stilled and Drake was long gone.

Drake unbound the boy two hours later in a dockside alley, in the backseat of his car. He called the binding sadist back from inside Thomas Myrdin's body and once again imprisoned him in his ring.

Drake pressed his hand over Myrdin's mouth to stifle his newly loosened screams.

"Quiet, or by the stars, I'll cut your throat. I assume you know who I am?"

"Zachary Drake." Myrdin's eyes filled with tears, his cheeks flushed red as his child's body tried to contain his fear.

"You understand that I've saved you from execution, yes?"

Myrdin nodded. Two fat tears rolled down his cheeks.

Drake felt suddenly very glad that he'd ordered tinted windows on his car. No passerby could fail to be disturbed by this scene. Fortunately, because of the madness of this night, he remained reasonably certain that no curious policemen would be peering through his windshield. Myrdin wiped his face on the now massive sleeve of his robe. His clothes were so big on him that he looked like he was wearing a nicely tailored duvet. The watch chain still dangled from his wrist like an undocked umbilicus.

"I don't know why you chose to intervene on my behalf, but I thank you, Grand Magician." His elegant words made an eerie counterpoint to his boyish soprano.

"Your thanks is not something I need."

"Then please tell me how I may repay you." Myrdin pulled the front of his robe closer around his chest.

"I can tell you that it's not with your scrawny body." Drake sat back and lit a cigarette. "I want your service."

"Service?"

"I will own you body and soul. That's fairer than you deserve for high treason, I assure you."

"If I refuse Louis will own my soul?"

"Louis?" Drake smirked at Myrdin's casual familiarity. "No, *Louis* will not own your soul. I have already obtained and destroyed your contract with the South Court. I refuse to deal in human souls. If I am to own you then you must sign the contract with me, yourself, of your own free will."

Myrdin's confusion clouded his soft pretty face.

"Are you saying that no one owns me right at this moment?"

"Just so."

"If I refuse, what will you do?"

"Then I will take you back to your execution, but you will face the axe a free man and you will not be owned against your will in death. It's as much as I can do for you."

Myrdin stared out the window. He asked for a cigarette and Drake gave him one. He pulled on it a few times, thoughtfully.

"Have you written the contract?"

Drake held up the paper by way of reply. He'd already signed it—a simple, one-page transaction, his signature in blood at the bottom. Myrdin finished his cigarette and threw the butt out the window.

"Do you have a razor?"

"When I remove this chain at your wrist there will be more than enough blood for your signature."

Myrdin nodded again and held out his wrist. Drake started to unwind the chain, careful to keep enough of Myrdin's blood trapped inside to seal their agreement. As Drake worked, the sounds of sirens became less frequent and the hard night turned a gray morning.

Finally, Myrdin signed the pact and Drake wrapped enslaving spells around his soul. Rather than fighting, he seemed almost relieved. Drake supposed that was because he was surprised to be even alive now to witness this daybreak full of wild animals and humans walking empty.

With Myrdin fully in his grip, Drake examined his soul, searching for a streak of evil that made him a child killer, preparing to strip him down, like Spider and Talon. He lacked a ring to house Myrdin, but that didn't matter so much. He could have Spider cocoon the soul until he got home. Myrdin's body could be donated at the hospital. There was always a dying child who deserved a second chance at life.

Drake pressed his awareness into Myrdin, who shuddered, but did not resist.

Inside, Myrdin felt sad.

Unusual for such a premeditated murder.

Drake searched for that black mark of evil and found only a sliver, far less than he imagined marred his own soul. More than that, he felt the oily residue of foreign magic. Drake drew back from Myrdin, confused. Could Myrdin be nothing but a pawn after all? But whose pawn was he?

Drake's heart sank as he realized he'd inadvertently thwarted another magician's plans and that that magician was almost certainly Everett. He'd imagined the goal of unleashing all this madness onto the palace grounds was to cover up his father's escape. Now uncertainty gnawed at him as he began to suspect another objective. It would be like Everett to use a proxy to achieve his goals and very much like Everett to conceal his more elaborate plans.

Drake said, "Tell me, did you go to Everett for this spell or did he approach you?"

"How did you know it was him?"

"It doesn't matter, does it?"

"I approached him but..."

"But?"

"I knew I needed to kill the baby, but she was enshrouded in protective spells that were beyond my capacity to break." Myrdin gazed out the window, the sadness Drake had felt inside him apparent on his face.

"You work magic?"

"I was in the academy until my parents were executed. The judge placed a three-generation ban on my family so I had to withdraw. I was a year ahead of you."

"Yes, of course, I remember you well." In truth, Drake's recollection of Myrdin was hazy, but the execution of Myrdin's parents remained vividly in his mind. All academy students had been required to attend so that they could understand the consequences of breaking magical law.

"I needed a trained magician to help me break through the spells surrounding the princess, but..." Myrdin looked down at his own childlike body, unable to express his bewilderment. "I don't know what happened."

"You have transfused your age into the princess. Around eighteen years, I think."

"I know that. I also know I didn't perform the ritual incorrectly, but the princess was supposed to die, not age. Everett obviously betrayed me, though the direction of his actions eludes me."

Myrdin's cold tone struck a wrong chord and Drake wondered if he would need to strip Myrdin down after all. "Have you no remorse for attacking the child?"

"I do, I..." Myrdin hung his head. Fresh tears slid down his cheeks. "I can't explain how it happened. I only knew that the princess would bring destruction to the city, at least I thought I did. It seems like a dream."

Drake nodded, contemplating this new information.

"So you left the academy while you were still in juniors?"

Myrdin seemed puzzled by Drake's change of subject but nodded. "When I was eleven."

"Are you aware of the concept of the sympathetic geas?"

Myrdin shook his head and Drake explained.

"Let's say I wanted the garbage taken out. If I put a sympathetic geas on that garbage, the first person who came across it and who had even the slightest desire to accomplish the task, would by their own amplified whim be compelled to take out my garbage for me." Drake offered Myrdin another cigarette and he took it, his small hand trembling as he began to understand. "I do not think you are, by nature, a child killer."

"It's not a cultivated habit, no." Again Myrdin's elegant phrasing rang at odds with his youth. "You're telling me that I've been used, aren't you? Because somewhere in my ugly soul I hated that little girl."

"That combined with your thwarted desire to be a magician. The geas required a person who wanted to work a spell, not merely an assassin."

"And you could see all this when we were in the throne room? That's why you intervened?"

"Not at all. I intervened because I thought your soul, being black as the starless void, would be of use to me."

"And now you see it's not." Myrdin kept himself under control, though his lip trembled.

"No, your soul is far too light for my purposes." Drake listened to the faraway sound of police sirens. Every emergency vehicle in the city seemed headed toward the palace grounds. The entire night had been one surreal catastrophe after another. Now he had this boy on his hands. He knew Everett hadn't meant for Drake to save Myrdin from execution. His own father had said as much. They'd meant to blame everything on the now diminutive scapegoat sitting in the passenger's seat.

He knew why Everett would release the Severing Wind. He plainly needed both a diversion and an event that would result in dozens if not hundreds of free-floating souls that he could capture. Everett must be planning to power a massive spell.

But this business with the princess perplexed him. Like Myrdin he could see no obvious immediate purpose to it.

Therefore it must be part of that larger spell.

"Then what, may I ask, are you planning to do with my soul?"

"Right now? Leave it in your body. I may still have some use for you. You will have to endure puberty again, I'm afraid." Drake shrugged. Now that he knew Myrdin to be a casualty of Everett's plan to free his father, Drake warmed to the boy. He felt like a servant ought to feel, humble, and with an edge of dependence that Drake found pleasing in a child. He decided that Myrdin needed a new name, or, failing that, needed to be released from his old one. "That doesn't matter now. From this moment you are no longer Thomas Myrdin. You are only Thomas, bound servant to Grand Magician Drake."

Again, that perplexing relief crossed Thomas's face. "What would you like me to do, my master?"

"First we will get you a haircut and some normal clothes, and then I need you to attend to a very important man."

"Who is that?"

"My father." Drake put the car into gear and made his way toward Everett's country house, rolling down alleys and across parking lots. Because of the mayhem at the palace, traffic was snarled and slow, and the gridlock provided ample time to explain Thomas's first mission.

"I know that Father and Everett are up to something, I just don't know what it is. I want you to inform me about the kinds of spells that they're doing. That should reveal something about their ultimate goal."

"But when Everett sees me he'll know that I know he's betrayed me," Thomas said. "And I feel certain he's not above murder."

"We'll simply have you play dumb. When you see Everett, or better yet, when you see my father, tell him that you tried to do the spell to kill the princess but got confused and messed it up. Neither one of them is likely to challenge that. Everett will believe that you think you made a mistake and that you do not suspect him. Trust me. He thinks that only a person who has been educated at the Royal Academy of Magic is capable of understanding spells."

"And you don't?"

"I've spent more time outside the palace than they have." Drake scanned the immobile line of vehicles in front of him then, seeing his chance, turned into a parking lot and wove through the parked cars to turn onto a less congested side street. "Magic is a capacity, not a diploma."

They fell silent again as Drake faced another tricky driving challenge. Thomas asked to turn on the radio and Drake nodded his permission. He scanned past live news broadcasts talking about lions roaming Tower Heights or detailing which lords and ladies had lost their souls.

In the less crowded suburbs, Drake stopped at a discount store and bought shorts, flip-flops and a T-shirt for Thomas. He also bought a pair of scissors. He lopped off Thomas's long blond locks in the parking lot and dumped them as well as

Thomas's bloodied court attire into the beige plastic garbage can that lurked near the discount store's entrance.

As they approached Everett's estate house, Drake thought he could see Thomas's hand shaking. He truly feared for his life. Even after everything that had happened today, he had not lost his capacity to be afraid.

Drake turned to him.

"Listen, even if Everett doesn't believe your story there is no way you will die. If he kills your body, I have hold of your soul and I have never lost my grip on what is mine." From the horrified expression on Thomas's face, Drake inferred that his words did not provide the comfort he had intended to imbue them with. "If your body is killed, I'll find you another. Bodies aren't hard to come by if you have connections and I—"

Drake's speech was cut short by Thomas laying his hand on Drake's shoulder.

"Please, Grand Magician, there is no need to reassure me further." Thomas's elegant cadence was at odds with his red shorts and cheap yellow T-shirt. "If I go to my death, it is nothing less than I deserve."

"Then let's go meet my father, shall we?"

Drake thought that if it was possible for a bird to look shocked, Sandy, Everett's cockatoo familiar, looked shocked at the sight of Thomas walking into the house. She let out a squawk, launched herself from her perch and flew up into the atrium of Everett's foyer to roost there with an assortment of other parrots and macaws. All inhabited familiars.

Her arrival set off a round of squawks and whistles, and he thought he could see one brilliant green parrot dialing a rotary phone situated in an alcove.

So he had only a couple of minutes until Everett knew Thomas was here.

"Is my father still in his rooms?" he called up to the bird as though her reaction had been perfectly reasonable.

"He's on the back lawn, annoying the crows. I'll show you to him." Sandy flapped her wings again, still flustered. She began to preen her wings in what looked like a nervous fashion. When she'd had a human body and worked as Everett's secretary she had the same habit of suddenly needing to smooth her hair when she felt anxious.

"Don't trouble yourself. Even if I hadn't lived here, I think I could still find the back lawn." Drake caught hold of Thomas's hand and pulled him along. Thomas's hand was ice cold.

"She's the one who brought me the pocket watch," he whispered.

"Don't worry. You'll be all right here, I promise."

He strode through the large, open doors and caught sight of his father. As Sandy had reported, his father seemed primarily occupied with annoying a set of crows trying to sun themselves on the wide green expanse of lawn. His father lurked at the edge of their circle, then suddenly rushed among them, scattering the birds into the air. He leapt after one of them, laughing a loud and barking sort of laugh.

Years spent living in a dog's body had apparently made a strong impression on him.

He caught sight of Drake and came striding toward him, heavily favoring his left leg.

"Zachary! You come back."

"Indeed, I have. I brought a young friend with me. This is my bound servant, Thomas, until very recently known as Lord Thomas Myrdin of the South Court."

Thomas gave an elegant bow. "It is my very great pleasure to make your acquaintance, Mister..."

"My name is Grand Magician Ignatius Drake, but you may call me Iggy." He seized Thomas's hand and shook it in the exaggerated, clownish fashion that he had always reserved for interactions with children. "But I believe you'll find that we are already well acquainted, young Thomas."

"We are?" Thomas looked to Drake, who shrugged his ignorance.

"You smuggled me out of the South Court, and for that I am forever grateful." Iggy executed a proper formal bow.

"You're the spirit who inhabited the terrier!" Thomas broke into a wide and charming grin.

"But what in the world has happened to you?" Iggy laid his hands on Thomas's shoulders.

"I had a little bit of a nervous breakdown," Thomas said.

"He tried to assassinate Princess Julianna," Drake put in, coldly.

Watching the concern spread across Iggy's face, Drake could not help but feel jealous. Seeing the two of them standing there was like watching a scene that had never occurred in his own childhood. He began to wonder over his choice to bring Thomas here. If he was going to have this sharp and aching envy, maybe it would be better to keep them apart.

But then who would spy for him?

No, Thomas needed to stay. Drake had to understand what his father had planned.

"You were the one who made the assassination attempt?" Iggy searched Thomas's face. "That doesn't sound like you."

"I wasn't in my right mind. Anyway it didn't work. Something went wrong with my spell and I ended up

100

transfusing my age onto her." Thomas hung his head in shame that Drake suspected was genuine. "I should have never tried to work magic."

"Well, it is a tricky business." Iggy ruffled Thomas's hair, his demeanor that of a father consoling a son after his team lost a big game. On the one hand Drake was glad that their lie had worked. On the other, he felt vaguely horrified that his father could forgive attempted infanticide so easily.

Then again, maybe his father knew Everett had initiated a geas and understood Thomas to be blameless. Or maybe—again that strange envious pain closed around Drake's heart—maybe his father just liked Thomas.

After all, they'd known each other for a long time.

Apparently.

"It's fortunate that the two of you are already well acquainted." Drake readjusted his sunglasses, glad the dark lenses hid his eyes. "I brought him to assist you."

"I really don't need an assistant, Zachary."

"Well, at the moment I can't keep him at my place. He's too recognizable. I was hoping you'd help me out," Drake said.

"It's dangerous for anyone to be with me right now, let alone a child."

"Not as dangerous as it is to be a condemned assassin in the proximity of the royal palace. And he's not a child. He's just in a child's body."

Iggy's mouth set in a grim line. Thomas merely kept his head down and his arms straight at his sides in a posture of abject shame. Iggy's expression softened and Drake took the opportunity to wheedle.

"In a couple of months no one will remember what he looks like and I'll be able to bring him back."

"Is this all right with you, Thomas?" Iggy asked.

Thomas lifted his face to Iggy. "I would feel safe with you."

Either Thomas possessed legendary acting skills or he spoke the absolute truth. Whichever was the truth, his words had an immediate effect on Iggy. The old man stood straighter and wore an expression of resolute confidence.

"Then I would be happy to have you."

Iggy ordered iced coffee and cookies from a passing bird, and he and Thomas began immediately to reminisce about their experiences at South Court.

Drake took his leave of them shortly thereafter, pained by their familiarity.

As he walked through the atrium, he glanced up. Spying Sandy looking down at him, he dug into his tight pocket for Everett's pocket watch.

"I think Everett dropped this." As he tossed the timepiece into the air, Sandy launched herself down.

He didn't bother to see if she managed to catch it or not.

Drake reached his Tower Heights home just in time to help zookeepers capture the roaming lion who had taken up residence in his condo building's lobby.

Chapter Seven

In the week following the catastrophe, vacant bodies roamed the city streets night and day. Posters went up on walls all through the civil sector as relatives of palace guards and servants searched for their loved ones. Other posters went up too, offering rewards for the return of this or that immortal soul. Scalpers did good business, but it was not as brisk as Drake would have expected. Dozens of souls had gone missing with no ransom ever being asked. That was not the work of scavenging amateurs gleaning their webs.

Soul catching on that level could only be accomplished by a grand magician, and Drake was left to wonder whether the culprit was Everett or his father. Not that they were the only two magicians capable of such a feat. Far from it, but catching and holding so many souls required planning, and they were the only two who had known the East Court medallion would be cracked. Probably they were splitting the catch between them, using it to fuel whatever new illegal deed they conspired to accomplish.

That they conspired was clear. Only one question remained: What was their goal?

Drake had not seen his father since he handed young Thomas over to him. When his father at last phoned, he claimed to be in the White Mountains in a lodge, hiding. Drake didn't believe him. When he tried to view his father remotely he found the image masked from magical sight. The old man had clearly discovered and eradicated Drake's own tracer spell, damn him. However, his father had forgotten to obfuscate the image of young Thomas, and so when Drake conjured up his newest servant, he saw the boy assisting his father with some mechanical object in a garage. Thomas then walked down the block to a convenience store. The signpost indicated the cross streets Bleeker and 237th. Drake's father was holed up in the suburbs, not far from where his servant, Nancy, rode out the crisis snuggled into her sister's guest room.

Drake watched Thomas drop a coin in the payphone outside and waited for the inevitable buzz of his own cell.

"I don't have much time," Thomas began.

"You're at a convenience store on Bleeker wearing red shorts with white piping and a T-shirt with a big yellow dump truck on it. Who are you letting dress you?"

"You know very well." Thomas's voice bristled with affronted dignity. "And I happen to like dump trucks."

"Maybe you can buy one with the money from your paper route," Drake said, snickering. "How is my father?"

"Iggy seems in good spirits, but he has a cough that he should see someone about and his left knee's very bad. I don't think the company that leased his body kept it in very good condition."

"And Everett?"

"He's been by once. To my face he apologized for the spell going wrong. He claimed senility, if you can believe that. And behind my back he told your father he didn't like me being here. Your father insisted I stay. We spent so much time together in the South Court and I think he's quite fond of having a child around. My suspicion is that he must be transferring his affection for you on to me since he was imprisoned when you were about the age I appear to be now. I have blond hair, of course, but that doesn't stop him from calling me 'Zachary' at least once a day."

Thomas's matter-of-fact observation of his father disarmed Drake, undermining his sense of ownership. He almost asked if his father ever talked about him, then restrained himself. Thomas didn't need to know how insecure he actually felt.

"I was more curious about the magic my father was doing, though I appreciate you looking after his health."

Thomas's lips compressed and he looked at the phone with slight scorn.

"He isn't doing much magic, as his health is not good enough to sustain large spells. Soulless-body servants are worked quite hard and not taken care of as they should be. Mainly we're harvesting souls from the nets Everett set up before he cracked the east medallion. I think your father knows why they're collecting and storing souls, but he isn't telling me what it is."

"Keep watching them then. And I'll keep watching you."

Again Thomas gave his phone receiver a look, this time a disgusted one. "Thank you...I think."

After he hung up, Thomas went inside and bought a box of taffy, apparently having already discovered "Iggy's" love of the stuff.

Drake let the image of Thomas go and went to his own cupboard to see if he had any candy of his own. Nothing. His refrigerator was equally barren of food, except for some beer and condiments. His freezer held nothing but stale ice and a couple of frozen dinners Nancy had left for him. He'd advised her to take a vacation until the unpleasantness at the palace had been sorted out. He'd felt benevolent and wholly unlike himself.

Now Drake found he missed Nancy.

He felt her absence most keenly at mealtimes when hunger forced him to venture out into the cordoned-off streets in search of sustenance. Tower Heights, his neighborhood, had been cleared of both wildlife and the roaming soulless days before. Every day he noticed another face missing from his routine. Being so close to the palace, and hence to the epicenter of the event, Tower Heights had suffered a massive depopulation. Posters depicting the missing abounded, as loved ones searched for lost bodies or severed souls.

This morning's prominent missing soul belonged to Marcel, the barista whose macchiato Drake preferred and on whom Drake had a fleeting crush the previous summer. His crush had withered when he saw Marcel's wife, pregnant and massive as a houseboat in dry dock. Now Drake watched her make his coffee, thin and ashen, glancing at him when she thought he wasn't looking, working up her courage.

Drake waited, anticipating her question, dreading it and also perversely wanting it.

As she handed Drake his coffee, her eyes dropped to the countertop. She'd lost her nerve. Drake lingered at the counter, taking his time situating the change in his wallet. He would not offer his services to her, could not bring himself to do it, but if she asked...

She did not ask. Her silence filled the empty coffee shop. Drake turned away and finally she spoke. "Grand Magician! Wait!"

He faced her again, taking in her stricken face, her green contact lenses.

"Yes?"

Under the full weight of his attention, words failed her again.

How different she is from the courtiers who I tried to warn the previous week. How afraid she is of my rejection.

She swallowed and came out from behind the counter.

"My husband, Marcel, he's..."

"Empty?" Drake supplied when her strangled pause became too long. She nodded and he continued, "And you want me to find him?"

"Yes, please." Her voice reduced to a whisper.

"Are you prepared to pay me?"

"Yes." Her answer came without hesitation, without even asking a price.

"And you agree to keep silent about our arrangement, now and ever after?" Excitement quickened Drake's pulse.

"Yes."

"Then give me your wedding ring," he said.

She complied, confusion showing on her face.

He searched the inside for an inscription and found it. "Is this a traditional ring?"

"Mrs. Riley made it at her forge." She pointed toward the jewelry store at the end of the block. Drake raised his eyebrows. Mrs. Riley had forged his own rings.

"And so you both added three drops of blood?"

"We wanted to do it right."

"And you did." Drake slid her ring onto his smallest finger, where the little diamond sat incongruously next to Spider. "I will see what I can do. In the meantime, make sure to keep the body hydrated."

"Marcel's body?"

"Yes," Drake amended, embarrassed at his own apparent callousness. "Keep Marcel hydrated."

"But you think you can find his soul?" Her expression lifted, inflated by hope.

"If his soul still exists in this realm I can find it. But much remains to be seen. Good day."

He left the coffee shop invigorated. He could not oppose the magics wrought by Everett or his father without feeling the cold grip of disloyalty around his heart. But now—now he had purpose. To find Marcel he must investigate and even go so far as to oppose their activities. His first stop would be the Museum of Magical Arts, only a few minutes walk from his condo. He grinned widely, so absorbed in his own thoughts that he nearly collided with Adam Wexley as he rounded the corner.

"Grand Magician!" Adam wore high-end athletic gear and looked flushed and sweaty. "I've been looking for you."

"More work from Lady Langdon? I'm afraid I'm on my way to the museum, but you can walk with me if you like."

He started down the hill toward the center of town and the great dome of the Museum of Magical Arts. Adam tagged along, his manner uncharacteristically cagey. His eyes roamed the street with paranoid intensity.

"I wanted to ask about the boy you took." Adam kept his voice low. "Thomas Myrdin."

Drake was disappointed that Adam had come to him only because he searched for another man. But his disappointment didn't last too long. The events of the past few days had shone the light of perspective on his infatuation with Adam. His chest still hurt when he looked at him; he still wanted to kiss Adam's mouth and at the same time, he felt the smallness of the problem of his unrequited feelings compared to the massive, and possibly deeply evil plots being hatched by his own father. It helped Drake to not feel too bitter.

"Fear not, Myrdin is perfectly safe."

"I saw you," Adam whispered.

"Saw me?" Drake couldn't bring himself to feel alarmed by Adam's conspiratorial tone. Only curious.

"I saw you push your ring into his neck. His mind wasn't destroyed at all, was it? You lied."

"It hardly matters now." Drake waved the accusation aside. "Myrdin's better off my servant than dead, wouldn't you agree?"

"But why did you do it?" Adam caught his arm. "What is he to you?"

Drake looked pointedly at Adam's hand on his arm and Adam released him immediately.

"To me? Thomas Myrdin is nothing."

"Then why?"

"Lord Wexley—"

"Please call me Adam."

"Adam. Not all magicians have intricately wrought plans for world domination. Some of us are simply workmen whose decisions are governed by what we feel is right at the moment. I wanted Myrdin to have a second chance. That's all."

Adam did not believe this explanation, Drake could see it in the set of his jaw. Yet he surprised Drake by taking him at his word. "Why do you think he deserves a second chance?"

"Don't you?"

"He tried to kill the princess. It's unforgivable!"

"So many things are unforgivable," Drake said, sighing. "I can't be expected to hold a grudge every time one noble has transgressed against another. So often they have been guided by unseen hands."

"By magicians, you mean?"

"I mean by politics, pacts, loyalties and, indeed, perhaps even by magicians."

"Do you think that's why he tried to kill her?" Adam searched Drake's face, clearly wanting his answer to excuse Myrdin's actions and allow him to keep his pristine image of "Lord Sapphire".

Jealous as he was, Drake couldn't take that from him.

"Between you and I, yes, I think that was the case." Drake lit a cigarette and offered Adam one, which he declined. He stood, smoking on the quiet street for a couple of minutes. Adam seemed to be digesting his words. Presently, he pointed to the diamond ring on Drake's pinkie. "You have a new ring."

"It's not mine." Drake laughed at the notion that he would purchase a tiny golden ring like this for himself. "It contains the blood of a soul I'm trying to retrieve."

"One that got knocked out of a body when the Medallion of Amabel cracked?"

"Just so."

"How will you find it?"

"I'm not sure yet. I have to do a little research."

"Can I help?"

Drake regarded him, puzzled by his request, and also suspicious. "Wouldn't that be taking you away from your duties to the West Court?"

"All they want is for me to be out of the way so they can do their work. But I want to help someone. I thought maybe that someone was you."

"So you didn't just come to ask about Lord Sapphire?"

"I wanted to know about him but I thought..." Adam looked confused, as if he could not divine his own reasons. "I thought you might put me to work."

Drake had worked so long alone that he couldn't begin to imagine what duty he would bestow upon Adam, yet the young courtier's sincerity moved him. And Drake did want him around.

"Come along then." Drake started moving and Adam fell in step beside him, happy.

Myrdin was on the roof of Danby Auto Parts, a squat two-story brick of beige concrete blocks. He stood in the dying sun holding a test tube and a rubber stopper. The heat from the flat tar roof soaked through his flip-flops.

Grand Magician Ignatius Drake, or Iggy as he had been instructed to refer to him, was gleaning his net. He pulled the entire thing down, like a fisherman hauling a catch aboard. The souls trapped within fluttered and writhed like strange fireflies. Myrdin's job during this process was to hold the test tube where the soul would be stored and, once Iggy had inserted a soul, to cork the top while whispering a simple spell.

"You don't want too complex of a spell right now because we'll just be opening these back up to strip them down later," Iggy explained.

Once the test tube had been filled, Myrdin put it in a special rack that Iggy had bought from the scientific supply store.

"Good work, Tom," Iggy told him. "When you're older and you're doing this yourself, you'll use your own materials, of course. Everett tells me that Zachary uses some kind of cocoons. It makes perfect sense, you know, him using a metaphor from the insect kingdom. His mother was a natural scientist. I imagine you'll use some kind of art-based method. Folded paper, maybe. There is a sect of folded-paper magicians far to the south who are quite fierce."

"I don't think I'll be growing up to be anything other than a servant," Myrdin reminded the old man. "Grand Magician Drake is known to keep tight hold of his souls."

"Oh, I wouldn't be so sure about tales of Zachary's great cruelty if I were you. I've never seen him so much as swat a fly."

"But you also haven't seen him in a very long time." Myrdin spoke as gently as he could, a trick he'd learned from years of placating Louis. "I'm happy to learn whatever you teach me, but let's not delude ourselves about my bright future."

Iggy paused and regarded him, a sad smile on his face, before reaching out and ruffling his hair. For some reason, Iggy could not resist bestowing random hair rufflings on him and now Myrdin found himself pleasantly anticipating the touch.

"You're so unnerving when you talk like that. Anyway I'm an old man. Indulge me in my high hopes for your success, as I'm far too old to entertain realistic dreams of my own."

At the intersection where Tower Heights met the Royal District, city police had set up a checkpoint. Only residents and workers were allowed past. They inspected Adam's identification first, questioning him about his connection to the West Court and finally demanding to see a second form of identification to let him back into the Royal District. Drake stood by during this interaction, looking on with growing and obvious irritation while Adam explained that he didn't have one. Adam felt his neck turning red in embarrassment. Less than five minutes and he was already an impediment to Drake.

When the police claimed to need to radio the West Court in order to verify Adam's identity, Drake finally flashed his magician's ID. The policemen's faces changed from bullying to obsequious as they studied the inverse pentagram embossed into the card.

They moved aside, mumbling, "Have a good day, Grand Magician."

"After you." Drake gestured for Adam to precede him. The police did nothing to further hinder their progress toward the museum's white marble colonnade. Adam hadn't been to the museum since his school days and felt a rush of nostalgia walking between the towering columns toward the carved wooden doors of the entrance. He remembered being afraid of the dark wood inlaid with silver pentagrams. Daring his school chums to touch one then finally laying his sweaty palm against the cool metal when no one else would—just to prove that nothing would happen. And he remembered his slight disappointment when nothing did.

He could clearly recall the excitement of rushing inside and running, shouting with his friends. The group moved like one noisy entity from diorama to diorama until they were shushed by the apprentice magicians who solemnly studied in the vast, dull library. He wondered now if Drake had been one of those annoyed apprentices.

"How old are you?" Adam asked Drake as they stepped into the long hallway.

Drake took a moment to respond, as if he had to go on a lengthy internal journey to access the information.

"I'm twenty-eight. Why?"

"I was just wondering." Probably not one of the apprentices. He would have been too old. "It's been a long time since I've been here. I remember it being more lively."

"Before the police blockade it was. Ah, here comes Madame Gantry to intercept us."

Down the stairs she walked, a little like a stately column herself with a tall, gray beehive hairdo and white linen business suit. Madame Gantry was the Guardian of the City, charged with protecting the inhabitants from fire, flood and demonic insurrection.

Adam wondered if her locus of power was her hair, but then decided that probably wasn't likely. Or was it? He knew so little of magic it was hard to discount.

"Would it be possible to seal a soul inside your hairdo?" Adam whispered. Drake choked and tried to suppress his laughter but failed. He laughed, covering his mouth with his hand. The genuineness of Drake's expression surprised Adam, who had mostly seen the icy veneer of Drake's professional demeanor. This smile invited. Adam wondered what it might be like to make love to Drake, what his sensual smile would look like, whether he would cover his face like he was doing now, trying to hide his reactions.

Madame Gantry reached them by that time and Drake's giggles dissolved beneath her stern gaze.

"You seem in good spirits." Her tone reprimanded but her expression remained pleasant.

"Madame Gantry, have you had the pleasure of meeting my friend Lord Adam Wexley? He's of the West Court."

Madame Gantry arched her gray eyebrows.

"I have not." Madame Gantry extended her hand and Adam shook it. Her fingers were intensely cold. "Although I've heard your name linked with Drake's quite often in the last few days. You helped him liberate the princess, isn't that right?"

"I'm afraid I didn't do much," Adam replied. Madame Gantry wasn't the first person to question his association with the grand magician. The persistence of Lady Langdon's interest in their association had begun to unnerve him. "I just happened to be there."

"And now you just happen to be here." Madame Gantry's silken comment confused him. Adam's bewilderment became more intense when Drake suddenly laced his fingers with Adam's and leaned in so that their shoulders brushed against each other.

"We can conceal nothing from you, can we?" Drake smiled at Madame Gantry.

"What would there be to conceal? Besides your cradle-robbing, I mean?" Her smile softened and she looked relieved, as though she'd been waiting for ages for the opportunity to tease Drake.

"I'm not that much younger—" Adam began, but cut himself short when Madame Gantry raised a silencing hand.

"Do you hear that?" she whispered, more to Drake than him.

"Birds." Drake's voice was soft.

"We should go to my sanctum," Madame Gantry went on in a hushed tone.

Adam expected Drake to release his hand, but he did not. He kept hold of Adam all the way up the stairs, only letting go when they passed through the brass-plated door into Madame Gantry's sanctum.

A miniature city spread out across a massive table, the buildings laid out in intricate detail. He reached out to touch the tip of the Black Tower but Drake intercepted his hand.

"This model is Madame Gantry's locus. You don't want to put it out of alignment."

"I'm sorry," Adam stammered, abashed. But he noted that again, Drake had hold of him. Probably trying to keep him from inappropriately prodding anything delicate.

Madame Gantry placed her hands gently on the table, near the palace, an intense look in her eye.

"Quickly, why have you come?"

"I need to consult *The Book of Demons*," Drake said.

Madame Gantry shook her head. "Not here. The birds will see you."

"I must consult that book." Drake's hand tightened around Adam's and Adam reflexively squeezed back.

"Please, Madame, someone's life depends on it," Adam entered the conversation. Both Drake and Madame Gantry stared at him curiously as if they'd forgotten he had the capacity for speech.

"When a grand magician needs to consult the book, it's safe to say that many lives depend on it," Madame Gantry finally said. Then, to Drake, "I will send the book to you at your house this evening."

"Thank you," Drake whispered. "I'm in your debt."

"You may add it to your bill." Madame Gantry walked back to the stairs and spoke loudly enough for her voice to echo through the empty hallways. "Please feel free to enjoy your romantic interlude in the museum, Grand Magician. Pray, give no thought to the chaos of the city or the good works you might accomplish with your skills. Indeed, trouble yourself not to think beyond the carnal pleasures of this summer afternoon."

"You know that I never do." Drake bowed slightly to Madame Gantry. Adam followed suit. He expected Drake to give up his grip and exit the building, but Drake didn't. Rather, he pulled Adam deeper into the museum, appearing carefree, commenting casually on the dioramas. Adam followed suit, careful not to glance up at the birds he knew peered at them from the skylights. Inhabited birds, certainly. Spying. But whose birds, and why?

Drake stopped beside the largest display, laid out on a wide, low pedestal in the center of the room.

"It's the palace grounds," Adam commented. "Except without the labyrinths."

"It's a model of the palace grounds at the time of the founding of our nation. See, here are the four seals, each containing one of the four great powers." Drake pointed to one monument that resembled a rough-hewn obelisk on the eastern side of the model. "This is the obelisk that houses the eastern medallion, also called the Medallion of Amabel. It contains the Severing Wind, which has power to separate body from soul."

"The one that cracked open last week?"

"The very same. There is one medallion in each court. Each contains the soul of one of the four Primary Magicians."

Adam leaned forward till his nose almost touched the glass dome covering the diorama. He knew this. Everyone did. He knew the first King Simon. Two of his brothers and two of his sisters came together to usurp the power of their cousin, Dunstan the Terrible, and his demon minions. The four siblings sacrificed themselves, allowing their souls to be stripped down into their strongest magical abilities and bound into the four medallions so that Simon could wield them as weapons. With the power of their souls fueling his sword, Demonslayer, he forged this city, this nation.

"I wonder how Amabel feels now."

"Happy, probably. Bound souls like to be released now and then. She's only been released two or three times since Simon smote the demon minions of his cousin."

"And with the defeat of the demons our modern state was born," Adam intoned.

"Something like that. Let's hope that no one else gets any grandiose ideas about harnessing primordial powers. We already know it doesn't end well."

Realization dawned within Adam. All this talk about King Simon and ancient history was Drake's way of explaining why they were here. "Then whoever cracked the medallion—"

Drake leaned close and kissed him on the cheek, whispering as he did. "Remember the birds."

Adam fell silent, admiring Drake's cunning.

They passed another hour in the museum, Drake pointing out this and that. Here was the surprisingly small armor of King Simon, hundreds of years old and shiny as the day it was made. There were the articulated bones of a massive leviathan, a demon servant of Dunstan, thirty feet from nose to tail with teeth longer than his hand.

"My mother worked on that skeleton. She helped Madame Gantry reassemble it. She was a paleontologist."

They quit the museum near four o'clock when the summer mugginess constricted the air. The sidewalks reflected back the heat. Sweat trickled down Adam's chest beneath his shirt as they walked back up the hill to Drake's condo to wait for Madame Gantry's delivery. A tan young lady bearing a strong physical resemblance to Madame Gantry arrived just after twilight to deliver a musty book as big as Drake's torso, hidden in a rolling suitcase.

After she'd gone Drake immediately hefted the tome and handed it to Adam.

"Follow me." Drake led Adam into his bedroom, stopping only briefly to acquire an old telescope and stand. The drawn curtains and ruckled bedclothes gave the space the aura of a

118

hotel room on the morning after. "You can put the book down on my bed."

For a moment, Adam thought this whole afternoon had been some kind of elaborate come on. And though he knew it wasn't, he still felt deeply awkward standing there looking at the top of Drake's mahogany nightstand, empty except for a box of tissues and a saucer of what appeared to be water.

"Shall I open the drapes?" Adam asked.

"No, we want to avoid attracting attention. Especially from birds." Drake fitted the old telescope with an almost blackened lens and beckoned Adam over. Carefully, he parted the drapes so that the telescope lens just poked through. "What I need you to look for is a red flicker hanging in the sky. If you point the telescope over Goddess of Mercy Hospital you can see one."

Peering through the lens was like seeing a circle of night in the middle of the day. As Drake predicted, a red aura flickered over the hospital.

"And there are souls in that net?"

"Probably. Don't ever die in a public hospital if you can help it." Drake flopped down on the bed behind him. Adam heard the old book bounce. "Now that you know what you're looking for I want you to scan the area surrounding the palace grounds for flickers like that. Try to use averted vision."

"What's that?"

"The method by which you can see very faint stars. Fix your eyes on one point and then concentrate on what you see out of your peripheral vision."

Adam did as instructed, his excitement growing. Averted vision. That was just the kind of quasi-mystical jargon he'd expected from a grand magician. He warmed to Drake again, as he had in the museum, when Drake had laughed so unexpectedly. Of all his acquaintances, only Drake cared to put

119

Adam to work. Only Drake had not disregarded his desire to help. And since Drake had accepted him, curiosity about magic burned within Adam where none had existed before, simply because Drake allowed questions.

"But would Marcel's soul still be there? It's been almost a week since the incident."

"Contrary to popular belief, it takes quite a long time to strip a harvested soul down to a useable form. There's a good chance that Marcel hasn't been processed yet. The trick is to find him."

Resolved to doing just that, Adam moved his eye purposely over the palace skyline, suspicious of every glint from a sliding glass door. Averting his vision, checking again.

He heard Drake open the book and immediately smelled the ancient leather pages.

"It smells like a funeral home," Adam said.

"It's the preservatives. This book is written on human skin."

Adam shuddered inside, his lip curling in disgust. "Why does magic have to be that way?"

"Which way?" Drake sounded distracted and vaguely bored.

"Degrading." Adam left off scanning the horizon to face Drake. The magician had donned a pair of reading glasses with ruby-red lenses and held the enormous book open across his lap. "Everything about magic degrades people."

"Not everything about magic degrades people." Drake pushed the glasses atop his head and lifted his hand to display the incongruous ladies wedding ring he wore. "This magical item forges a bond between two people that is strong enough for me to use it to pull Marcel's soul out of a soul net. I don't find that degrading."

"But so many other things do." Adam waved to *The Book of Demons*. "Especially this. Why did it have to be written on human skin?"

"Because it was written by demons who didn't regard humans as being equal to them, which I find interesting, since most of the demons who wrote this tome started off in human form."

"They did?"

"Certainly. Listen, you won't see anything until it gets a little darker. Come sit." Drake patted the bed next to him. "I'll read while you wait."

Adam lowered himself onto the mattress next to Drake and took a deep breath before looking, with some trepidation, at *The Book of Demons*. The deep-brown pages appeared to be traced with lighter pink lines, like line drawings made of scars. Adam imagined instantly and vividly how this book must have been manufactured—each page cut into a living body then harvested after the image had healed. Revulsion filled him.

"There aren't any words."

"Of course there are, you just need these." Drake situated his glasses on the bridge of his nose. After studying the page, he remarked, "This old-fashioned writing is so hard to read."

"Why do you need this book, anyway?"

"I need to find out the exact method for cutting between this world and the ghost realm."

"Are you going to do it?" Adam asked.

"No, I think someone else is going to do it. I thought you got that while we were at the museum."

"I did, but then I wasn't sure. So these people, are you going to stop them?"

Drake's mouth tightened to a grim line. "So long as I'm not inconvenienced, it's not any of my business what other magicians do."

"Then why are you trying to find out?"

"Because I think it very well might inconvenience me." Drake flashed Adam a smile, and then turned his attention back to the book. "Here the writer describes the method for inhabiting the body of a demon. It's almost exactly like inhabiting an animal, except that the demon's soul must be removed before the magician's soul can invade. Severing a demonic soul from its body takes tremendous power."

"So whoever has Marcel is going to use him to sever a demonic soul?" Adam asked. Drake shook his head.

"No, Marcel is most likely being used, with a lot of others, to power some mechanism that will puncture the membrane between our worlds and allow a demon to come through in the first place." Drake flipped through a couple more pages, looking like a university student cramming for a test. A faint sulfur smell wafted up from the turning pages. "Here we go, it says, *As the Ghost Star ascends in the heavens, the membrane separating our two worlds grows thin. Any man not a coward, nor fearing damnation can crown himself the Demon King.*"

"That doesn't sound good," Adam murmured. Drake made no reply. The grand magician's hands had gone limp on the pages and a shadow of fear passed over his face. "Grand Magician? Are you all right?"

"I wish you would call me Drake." The grand magician apparently recovered himself and smiled at Adam, a guarded, professional smile. Dismissive by nature. Adam returned to the window.

"I don't see how this helps Marcel, Grand Ma—" Adam paused before he amended, "Drake."

"It helps me get a grasp of how many other souls might be trapped with him."

"If they're all together in a net then we can just free them all, can't we?"

"Not without their harvester noticing." Drake leaned close to Adam to peer out through the crack in the curtains. Adam could smell his woody cologne. Drake pushed the ruby glasses up on top of his head again. "Try searching out there in the northern suburbs."

Adam did as he was told. Within a couple of minutes, he saw the net flickering like an aurora in the sky. Drake double-checked Adam's findings and opened the window. Distant traffic noise floated up from the street. Drake dipped Marcel's wife's wedding ring in the saucer of water on his nightstand. He then whispered a few words, before pressing his lips to the ring and blowing out a kiss.

For a second Adam thought he could see the kiss blowing over the rooftops, fluttering like a moth.

"What did you do?"

"I sent out a little spell. If Marcel is in the net, the spell should find him. When she does, she'll wrap a little line around him and hopefully, I'll be able to reel him back."

"And after that?"

"We reinstall Marcel in his body. But it could take all night for my spell to find him. Are you sure you wouldn't find some other location more diverting?" Adam shook his head and Drake continued, "Or you could watch the television. I'm afraid I only get three channels, though."

Drake returned to his perusal of *The Book of Demons* and the shadow of fear returned to his face. Adam slumped down next to Drake on the bed, concerned. On an impulse, he reached out and patted Drake on the back. The magician tensed. Adam watched the hairs on Drake's neck stand up and his skin flush red.

He'd meant to comfort Drake, but when Drake looked at him the tension between their two bodies overwhelmed his gentler urges. Adam lightened his touch, made it more sensual than soothing.

"I can think of something more entertaining than television." The sudden, blatant invitation surprised even him, but he didn't retract it. He studied Drake's expression as it moved from confusion to temptation before the magician laid both the book and his ruby glasses aside.

"I should stay beside this window. It's where my spell will return."

"We'll stay here then." Adam stroked Drake's shoulder, feeling the fineness of the other man's bones, the compact sinews of his muscles, different from Adam's own gym-conditioned deltoids. Drake allowed Adam to unbutton his shirt and pull it aside. While Drake hadn't abused his body, he'd clearly spent no time worshiping the summer sun. His skin stretched pale and white over sinewy muscle. Adam traced the line of Drake's spine with his finger and Drake leaned back into his touch and laid his left hand on Adam's thigh—his first reciprocation.

"I should take a shower."

Adam pressed his lips against the back of Drake's neck. "We can do that after."

He pulled Drake against his chest, fitting their bodies together, wrapping his arms around him. He could feel Drake's pulse pounding in his chest and see the veins of his throat jump. Again Adam felt his own physical power overwhelming the reticence of Drake's intellect. He resolved not to let Drake talk much, sensing that that other man would try to distance himself from the heat rising between their bodies with a barrage of deflating words.

The trick would be to give his mouth something nicer than speaking to do.

Adam sought Drake's lips and found them open to him, softly pliant, almost passive. Curious to see how far he could take his own dominance, Adam sought out Drake's nipple and pinched it to hardness before smoothing the sting away. Drake gasped then relaxed further into him, giving up any pretence of leadership, allowing Adam to undress him, direct him onto his back, keep him there while Adam unrolled the latex. While Drake lay there, exposed, knees raised and legs apart he turned his face away, hiding behind one hand, just as Adam had suspected he would.

"Can you turn off the lamp?" Drake murmured into the pillow.

Adam complied and moved into position, placing himself right at Drake's entrance, beginning to push.

That Drake hadn't made this kind of love in a long time became immediately evident, but Adam took his time, coaxing and encouraging him until at last he slid inside. He wished he could see Drake's face, but the evening light had gone. He could only hear Drake panting and slowly relaxing enough for Adam to begin the noble work of creating friction.

At first his movements could be measured in increments of an inch, but gradually Drake loosened enough to begin to meet his thrusts with equal force. Escalation came quickly as Drake began to moan and clutch at Adam's forearms. Adam pounded like a jackhammer, mumbling nonsensical phrases about how good Drake felt and how beautiful he was until at last ecstasy crashed over them.

Chapter Eight

None of Drake's spying or elaborate fantasies had prepared him for the reality of sex with Adam. If he'd been lewd, Drake would have known what to do. Drake could have gone farther, been more lascivious than him. It would have been a game of bravado and Drake would have won.

But Adam was different. He acted with intuitive skill that required no elaborate negotiations. And when he spoke, the sincere explicitness of Adam's compliments had made Drake shy.

Afterward Drake fell asleep, the kind of sleep that lazy dogs and babies enjoy. Exhausted, forgetful and sweaty.

When he opened his eyes, the sky was dark and his little moth-shaped spell rested on his pillow holding a tiny, nearly invisible thread of another spell, like a stray ray of moonlight, between its front legs.

"Have you found Marcel?" he whispered. The spell bounced and quivered in excitement. He reached out and lifted the thread, curling it around his finger once, twice. He tugged, feeling the resistance, the weight of Marcel's soul at the other end. The spell fluttered around his face as Drake sat up.

"Good girl. Come back home now." He offered his palm. The spell alighted and, like a snowflake melting, dissolved into a droplet of water that he returned to the saucer on his nightstand. Now full of the little spell's knowledge, the water showed where Marcel hung, trapped with a hundred other souls in a net above the intersection of Bleeker and 237th. His father's net. Drake saw him showing young Thomas how to hold the trapped souls until it was time to process them.

It didn't shock him. From the start he'd known that he'd be stealing from his father. Him or Everett, anyway. Drake's only concern was that his father would have ingested Marcel, forcing Drake to decide whether or not to try and pull Marcel out. Pulling a soul from inside a magician could be fatal to the magician. Drake was glad to not have to make the decision.

Already he worried that if his father and Everett planned the unthinkable crime of opening the demon realm, he would be the one to oppose them. He pushed that thought down. It had to be wrong. And there was nothing to do about it now, anyway, when Marcel still awaited his rescue.

Drake awakened Spider. She made her way along the underside of his hand and then lowered herself by a strand of spell silk to his nightstand. Feeling kind, he stroked her abdomen with his pinkie. In return, she bit him. Drake smirked, chagrinned by his Wexley-induced sentimentality. If Spider had been the sort of soul who could understand affection, she wouldn't be trapped inside that ring. Drake whispered, "Catch this soul for me," and fed her the end of the thread that she began to spin into a cocoon.

Drake wrapped the thread around his finger again and again, pulling a little harder each time, jiggling Marcel free of the net that held him. Glancing into the saucer of water on his nightstand, Drake could see the net where Marcel hung, drifting like a jellyfish through the clouds above the auto-parts store, its tendrils catching souls and pulling them up into a holding chamber.

Adam stirred at Drake's movement, but only to cuddle closer. He curled around Drake, planting a warm kiss on his hip. His muscular body felt as substantial as a recliner. Adam propped himself up on one elbow, yawning.

"What are you doing?" Adam's alertness returned all at once.

"Reeling in Marcel's soul." Drake saw on Adam's face the admiration that he craved, tinged with exuberant impatience.

"Let's go!" Adam was on his feet immediately.

"Go where?"

"To put Marcel back in his body."

"He's not here yet. I've got him at the end of this line."

Adam paused, confused, pants in hand. "What are you talking about?"

"You can't see it but it's in my hand. I'm feeding it to Spider and she's building a cocoon for us to carry Marcel's soul in."

For the first time, Adam seemed to notice Spider's work. Her movements clearly disturbed him. Drake wondered if he had arachnophobia. "Why don't you go make some coffee? I should have him by the time it's done."

"Are you sure you want me going through your kitchen?"

"I feel like we've reached at least an open-refrigerator level of intimacy."

Adam grinned like a little boy. He mashed a kiss into Drake's cheek and went off to explore the kitchen, naked, pants dangling from his hand. Drake watched him go, amazed by the sight.

Spider continued her labors while the smell of fresh coffee percolated through the condo. Stars lit the sky, but the air inside the bedroom stayed muggy and close. Drake opened the window and let the night breeze enter, finally unafraid of spying avians. No parrot flew at night. Nor any other familiar in Everett's collection.

Adam brought coffee and sandwiches just as Spider and Drake finished securing Marcel inside his cocoon. The whole package was only as big as the top of his thumb. When he let Adam hold it, Adam cradled the cocoon in his cupped palm, careful even of breathing too hard on it. While Adam showered and dressed, Drake drank a cup of coffee and ate the roast beef sandwich Adam had made. Drake took his turn afterward, their bodies brushing against each other as Adam stepped out of the shower and Drake entered. For a moment, Drake thought they'd make love again, then they both seemed to simultaneously remember their mission.

They returned to the coffee shop just before closing time. Marcel's body trudged around the dining room, sweeping the floor in the same lethargic manner that Drake's father had cleaned up cigarette butts when he'd been soulless. Marcel's wife approached them hesitantly, eyeing Adam with restrained suspicion.

"Grand Magician, I didn't expect you back today."

"I've come to return your property." Drake extended his palm. Her wedding band lay on his open palm, next to the cocoon. She didn't take either of them, only stared at the cocoon with confusion.

"What is it?"

"It's Marcel! He's inside." Adam burst in to the conversation, unable to control his glee.

"How do we get him out?"

"You don't. You put this"—Drake pointed at the cocoon then at the soulless Marcel—"in there. You might want to butter it up. Sometimes it's hard to swallow something that big."

Unlike Drake's own father, soulless Marcel was not a recalcitrant body. Explaining that the cocoon was medicine, Marcel's wife easily convinced him to ingest his soul. At his wife's urging, he obediently gulped down iced tea. It took him three tries and four glasses to completely swallow the cocoon. Then Drake observed a light of personality glimmer in his eye. His wife saw it too and she rushed forward into Marcel's embracing arms.

Drake left before they started thanking him. He had never been able to accept gratitude.

Adam caught up with him at the end of the block. He didn't ask why he'd left and Drake appreciated that.

"I told Amy and Marcel that you had a lot of other people to help."

"Who's Amy?"

"Marcel's wife. I don't think you'll be having to pay for your coffee anymore."

Drake marveled at how Adam, in just two minutes, had learned her name when Drake had never bothered in all the years he'd frequented their establishment.

"I don't think I'll be going there anymore anyway."

"Why not?"

"I don't like how people behave when they feel indebted to me."

"How do they act?"

"They pay too much attention to me." Drake paused thoughtfully. "Much like you're doing now."

"They just feel grateful now because you've saved Marcel's existence. It will wear off." Adam regarded Drake, then smiled kindly. "You're really shy, aren't you?"

"I am not shy." Even as Drake spoke he felt himself shrinking bashfully away from Adam. "How could a person who dresses like me possibly be shy?"

That settled it. He would pull Adam down this very alley and disprove this preposterous theory. His own confidence depended on it.

"Fashion isn't everything." Adam caught him around the waist and pulled him up close against his chest, like a dancer might hold a partner. Drake scanned the sidewalk for onlookers, but because of the curfew and the police checkpoints, the normally busy street was empty except for a couple of cats. And they didn't look inhabited. So he relaxed against Adam, hooked his thumbs in Adam's belt, and kissed him.

Drake drew back, leading Adam around the corner and into the dark alley. Drake dropped to his knees, massaging Adam's thighs, feeling Adam's cock hardening through his pants.

"What are you doing?" Adam whispered.

"Proving you wrong."

"Wrong about what?"

"My alleged shyness." Drake pulled the front of Adam's warm-ups down and Adam's cock bobbed free, undeterred by any sort of undergarments. Drake wrapped his hand around the base and took in as much as his mouth would allow. Adam moaned, hands in Drake's hair.

Then the phone in Adam's jacket pocket rang, vibrating against Drake's cheek. Drake almost choked then recovered, sucking hard, trying to ignore the sudden technological intrusion.

Adam made every effort to ignore the phone as well, but Drake could feel Adam's anxiety growing with each buzz. Drake released Adam's anatomy and gazed up at him. "Do you think it's your godmother?"

"No one else would call this many times in a row."

"Just answer it then."

"While you're doing that?"

"Consider it a challenge." Drake returned his attention to the task at hand, feeling his own excitement growing as Adam answered the phone and tried to speak clearly.

Adam listened, glanced down at Drake and then said, "I happen to be with the grand magician right now... I'll ask him."

"Ask me what?"

"If you'll come to the West Court immediately? The princess is possessed."

"Give me the phone."

Adam did as instructed. Drake spoke, his voice slightly rough.

"Lady Langdon, how lovely to hear from you."

"Grand Magician." Lady Langdon's strident, panicked voice filled his ear. "You must come—"

"Yes, I must." Drake nuzzled Adam's stomach. "I just have to finish something and I'll be right there."

Drake hung up and turned the phone off.

"Now where was I?"

"But the princess..." Adam's protests died as Drake renewed his efforts.

"She'll still be possessed when we get there."

The main feature of the princess's chamber at the West Court was a massive canopied bed, draped with buttercup-yellow and royal green silk. Stuffed toys and cut flowers

132

decorated every surface. Tall glass doors opened up to a balcony that had a stunning view of the Malachite Palace and its surrounding labyrinth, which was now badly damaged from the Night of the Severing Wind. The doors stood open, allowing cool night air to penetrate the hot room.

The princess lay on a narrow medical trolley close to the open doors. The young woman's hands and feet had been lashed to the bars on the sides. Though her body was that of an eighteen-year-old, her eyes remained those of an uncomprehending infant. Red scratches and purpling bruises covered what Drake could see of her exposed arms and legs. Her breath came in muffled whimpers that sounded both pitiful and revolting. The thick tang of urine hung in the air around her. Another young woman slept on the full-sized bed, Lady Carolyn, presumably. The only other occupants of the room were four silent soldiers. The green-cross badges on their uniforms identified them as army medics.

Adam went to the princess immediately, stroking her hair back from her face. "Poor little girl."

Drake put on his ruby spectacles and searched the room for spells.

He was not surprised to find his father's magic there, only shocked by the extent of it. He could feel magic at work everywhere in this room. Layer after layer of enslaving spells. He took some time to retrieve his cigarette case and lighter from his jacket pocket and made a leisurely show of lighting it while he collected his calm. Then he addressed Lady Langdon.

"And how long has Her Highness shown signs of possession?"

"Since around two this afternoon." Lady Langdon crossed her arms over her stomach. The previous week's strain showed on her face.

"Generally speaking, a possessed person should not be restrained," Drake commented. "Often the possessor will badly hurt the body trying to escape the bonds. The recommended course is to allow the possessed person to move freely, provided that they're in a secured room."

Lady Langdon looked stricken. "She kept crawling and trying to stand then falling. Her muscles aren't developed yet."

"Do you have any idea where she keeps trying to go?"

"She wants to go into the courtyard, as far as I can tell." Lady Langdon gazed at her granddaughter and her expression revealed the intensity of her pain and fear for the girl. Drake felt a pang of sympathy for them but already knew he could not intervene.

Anger flared up inside him and he swallowed it back down. Why was his father doing this? What revenge plot had he nurtured for all those years in that terrier's brain? Even as he thought it, he knew revenge wasn't his father's intention. In that case, why attack the royal family? No, their actions could have only one aim—a magical coup.

Drake realized he had to confront them. He turned to Lady Langdon. "I'm sorry, there's nothing I can do right now."

"What do you mean there's nothing you can do?" A note of hysteria colored her voice and Drake instinctively stepped back out of her reach. "You are the best magician in this city."

"Apparently, I am not." It hurt Drake to admit defeat in front of Adam. "I don't know how to counter this spell, but I'll look into it. Have you consulted the royal magician?"

"Everett?" Lady Langdon spat the name. "Yes, he's been here." Although she said nothing against Everett, her tone and hateful glare conveyed her suspicions about his mentor. Drake couldn't blame her, yet neither could he confirm her fears. Not before he spoke to his father. Lady Langdon wrapped her cold fingers around his arm and pulled him close. She looked Drake straight in the eye without blinking and spoke in a low whisper. "I assure you that I can adequately compensate you for your intervention in this matter. As much you want."

"It's not a matter of money." Drake didn't have to feign insult at her assumption that his reluctance constituted a form of bargaining. "Now I must go. I'm sorry."

Drake removed himself from her grip and started for the door. Adam's voice stopped him cold. "Can you really do nothing, Drake?"

Drake cringed to hear him call his name so familiarly in front of Lady Langdon.

"Not now...not yet." He turned back slightly and mumbled another apology before quitting the bedchamber.

"Don't go after him," Drake heard Lady Langdon say, presumably to Adam. "He's a coward. Let him go."

Adam didn't follow. Drake knew he wasn't Adam's hero anymore; the knowledge ached deep in his chest like an unexpressed sob.

He returned to his empty condo and fell into the bed they had shared, curling into a tight ball, trying not to think about how on the very first day he'd had Adam, he'd most likely lost him.

Directly after finishing his morning coffee, Drake hailed a taxi and spent the hour's ride from the Tower Heights to his father's lair fabricating a line of reasoning proving the inevitability of losing Adam Wexley, hoping to find comfort in contemplation of the fallacy called Eternal Love and growing increasingly morose. He felt a flare of nihilism rising up from the deep recesses of his subconscious.

If Everett and his father continued with their insane plan, he had so much more to contemplate than his faltering love life. Being prone to reflexive goodness and a desire to protect the heir, Adam wouldn't likely survive the initial attack. The only hope of saving him lay in stopping the plan before they went any farther.

His father showed no surprise when he arrived at the auto-parts store. Or if he did experience curiosity about how Drake had found him, he didn't show it.

"I was just about to send Tom to the convenience store for some sandwiches. They have cheese and black pickle." Iggy's voice implied that nothing could tempt Drake more.

Of course he would have to remember Drake's childhood favorites now, right when he was about to have an argument with him.

Drake glanced over at Thomas, who looked at the floor. "Do they have cinnamon pop?"

"Only Red Devil brand," Thomas said.

"Then get me one of those too—and some coffee sponge cake." Drake dug some cash out of his pocket and handed it to him.

Thomas looked to Drake's father for confirmation. Drake's father stuck his hands in his pockets, shrugging his helplessness.

"You're his minion, not mine," he said.

Thomas turned to Drake. "Can I have a smoke for the road?"

Drake tossed him the remainder of his pack. "Take your time coming back."

He watched Thomas go, then stood awkwardly alongside his father.

"You and he seem to be getting along well."

"I've known Thomas for a long time." Iggy sat down on a cheap folding chair. "I was already in the South Court when he arrived. I used to watch him painting. He's quite a good artist, you know."

"I didn't."

"Then he's not a close friend of yours?" Drake's father regarded him. A puzzled expression flitted across his face then vanished.

"Not at all," Drake replied. "I only know him because his parents were executed when we were in school."

"I assumed that was why you rescued him and brought him here."

"I just thought you'd need someone to help you. He owed me. That's all. But I'm not here to talk about Thomas. I was summoned to the West Court yesterday."

"Oh?" A hint of a smile tugged at the corner of his father's mouth. "Did you make some money?"

"The princess is possessed."

"Aren't they all, at some point or other? It seems to be the price they pay for primogeniture. A small price, considering that they will inherit our kingdom."

"I felt your magic there."

"And?" His father regarded him evenly.

"I came to ask you to stop." Though there was no one else in the building, Drake found himself unable to speak above an emphatic whisper. "I know what you and Everett are planning. It is total insanity."

"Speak plainly, Zachary." His father's demeanor remained easy, almost indulgent. "What do you think we're doing?"

"I think you're trying to usurp the throne." Drake wished he could raise his voice to a casual volume, but paranoia had him in its tense, sweaty grip.

"And if we are, who are you to complain? Everett has no children. You are my only son. For whom do you imagine we are acquiring this throne?" Drake's father's expression turned purely kind. "I wasn't able to give you anything while you were growing up. I didn't have a chance to teach you my magic. But I aim to make up for my past failings."

"You're trying to install me as king?" Drake stared stupidly at his father, who nodded. Drake asked, "Why would you do that?"

"I am doing my best to compensate for the many birthday presents I haven't given you over the years." His father chuckled. "What do you think? Is the malachite throne adequate compensation?"

The image of himself sitting on the malachite throne, ruling the four courts, was so wrong that he could not even conjure it. Anyone who knew him could have predicted his repulsion at the thought of rulership. And even though his father hadn't communicated with him for decades, surely Everett had known he would not want to be king. That if he rejected the notion of owning any soul not already condemned to death, owning entire armies of soldiers would disgust him.

Yet his father meant well. He saw it in his face, so proud of the fantastic gift he would shortly bestow upon Drake.

Looking into his eyes, Drake knew his father had no motivation beyond installing him as monarch.

But what of Everett? Drake did not believe for one second that Everett's only intention was to see Drake crowned king.

"I appreciate the thought, Father, but I am not well suited to rulership. And I would not want anyone to open up the gates to the demon realm on my account."

"Open the demon realm? Who said anything about that?"

"Why else would you need to amass a reservoir of souls?"

"To fight the royal magicians."

"Everett *is* the royal magician," Drake countered.

"But not every magician will support his ascension."

"So it's Everett who will be king?" This plan began to make more sense.

"Initially, but you will be his heir. That was our agreement," his father said. "Don't think that this plan is something Everett and I came up with yesterday. We've been talking for years."

"While you were a dog?"

"We developed a rather clever system of sign-language barks and growls," his father replied. "Sometimes hope of success was the only reason I didn't throw myself under a delivery truck—that and the infernal self-preservation instincts of that particular terrier."

"You're free now." Drake reached out and laid his hand on his father's shoulder. "You don't need the plan anymore."

"Are you saying you want me to stop?" His father asked in disbelief. "These are huge forces set in motion, Zachary. There will be repercussions."

"If you're doing this to make me king, then I am asking you to stop. Hundreds of innocent people will be caught up in this conflict and for what? Does Everett promise them a better future than the current monarch?"

"The people? I don't know what the people may or may not want or even need. I don't know that Everett offers them any long-ranging reforms, if that's what you mean." His father ceded his point, but Drake could see that it hurt him to do so. "But the future would certainly be better for Everett."

"How do you mean?"

"His soul is owned by the king. Don't you understand what that means?" Iggy's expression grew dark. Haunted.

"It means that he can be sold at any time, at a whim." Drake forced coldness into his voice. "Everett knew when he signed his soul into the service of the court that his soul was no longer his own. That is the consequence of royal magicians."

"Don't you have any heart at all, Zachary?" His father's eyes were furious now. Scornful. "Don't you understand that what happened to me happened because my soul was owned by the South Court? Can't you grant Everett the grace to try to change his circumstances?"

"It's not as though he hasn't profited from the arrangement. And it's not as though he doesn't own souls himself. He freely purchases souls whenever it suits him." Drake tried to keep himself steady, reasonable, but he found his voice incompliant. It rose in volume and force until he was nearly shouting. "He has no right to take the lives of others because he feels like he might have made a mistake."

In the face of his sudden emotional escalation, his father seemed confused, then somehow contrite. All anger seemed to have abandoned him. "So Tom was right after all."

"Tom?"

"He said that you would not comply with our plans for you. He told me you were famous in the court for your aversion to slavery and that everyone knew you couldn't be bribed or blackmailed into breaking the law. That's why he didn't even approach you about his plans for revenge, even though you were cute." His father winked at him and Drake felt his cheeks flush. What other choice facts had Thomas related to his father?

"I think that's a little bit of an exaggeration. Many courtiers think of me more as a coward than some kind of paladin." He fumbled in his pocket for his cigarettes before realizing he'd given his pack away.

"Even so, it means you're serious, doesn't it?"

"About not wanting the throne? Yes, I am. If Everett wants his soul back, it's not my place to hinder him. But if you two plan to resort to opening the demon realm, I will have no choice but to oppose you."

Drake's father regarded him for an excruciating moment and shook his head. He stuck his hands in his pockets, almost contrite. "How are you so much like your mother?"

Before Drake could answer, he felt the familiar buzz of his phone ringing. Emotionally overwrought and grateful for the interruption, he answered. Lady Langdon wanted to meet at his condo. She wanted to make a deal he couldn't refuse.

He told his father he had to go. Iggy nodded, resignation showing on his face. On an impulse Drake embraced him, throwing his arms around him like he had last week when he'd walked on four paws out of his elevator. His father squeezed him tight, then let go. "I wanted to give you something great."

"It's enough to have you back at all." Drake's voice broke on his last word. "We've lost so much time together, I don't want to lose more years waiting while you and Everett stage a pointless coup."

Taken aback, his father replied, "I'll always make time for you, Zachary."

Drake wanted to believe this was true, but his father had been free for days and the time they'd spent together could still be counted in minutes. So he simply nodded and left, too emotional to speak and too embarrassed to stay.

Myrdin returned with cake and soda, but Drake had already gone. Iggy slouched in a battered armchair in the corner of the dank living room. He looked old. His cut-off shorts seemed suddenly ragged instead of youthful. When he saw Myrdin he reached into his back pocket and pulled out his wallet.

"How much was our bet?"

"I bet fifty that Drake would refuse you." Myrdin laid the plastic bag of snacks on the coffee table. "Did I win?"

"Am I paying you?" Iggy sounded glum. To cheer him, Myrdin rubbed his hands together in an unnecessarily theatrical show of gloating. Iggy peeled off one bill, then another, then counted a stack of crumpled ones to equal the amount of their wager. He handed them to Myrdin, who stuffed them in the top pocket of his backpack. "That should keep me square with the tobacconist for quite some time. It's a pleasure doing business with you, sir."

"You shouldn't smoke, you know. Your lungs are tiny now." Iggy flopped his feet on the coffee table and leaned back, staring up at the stained ceiling.

"Yes, Mother, I'll take that under advisement."

"If you're going to be rebellious, you could at least call me Dad."

"You're just lucky I don't call you Fido." Myrdin offered Iggy a soda, which he accepted. After a few drinks Iggy shook his head.

"I just can't believe it. Zachary's as moralistic as a woman."

"I told you so."

"How could he have grown up like that?" Iggy continued in genuine wonderment. "Even his mother was less rigid."

"He hasn't lived in the court and so moral relativism hasn't been necessary to his survival. Are you still going ahead with your plan?"

"I don't see that we have much choice. Even if Zachary doesn't want the throne, which astounds me, let me assure you—"

"It is mystifying." Myrdin took a bite of his cake.

"But even if Zachary doesn't want the throne, Everett won't stop wanting his freedom. We've spent twenty years planning this." Iggy shook his head again. "Everett's going to be so disappointed in Zachary."

"Do you think he'll be all right?"

"Zachary? Of course. Everett could never hurt my son. He's taken an oath."

"A magical oath?"

"No, not a magical one." Iggy regarded Myrdin strangely. "Are you actually worried about Zachary's safety?"

"I just...I just think that Everett isn't telling you everything," Myrdin blurted out. "I'm worried that he's playing you like he played me."

"How do you mean he played you?"

"He told me that I was the Guardian of the City and put a geas on me so that I would do the spell that forced my age onto the princess."

"I thought you said you tried to kill her and made a mistake and youthened yourself by accident." Iggy sat forward in his chair.

"Drake—your son—told me to say that so that Everett wouldn't suspect that we were on to him. Did you really think I tried to kill a baby all on my own?" Myrdin wished his voice could be huge and deep with affront instead of the trembling, thin soprano that it had become.

"You were very angry at your boyfriend," Iggy pointed out. "He'd treated you badly for years."

"Being mad at Louis is insufficient motivation for me to turn into a baby killer!" Myrdin said, aghast. "For the stars' sake, Iggy, you've known me for years. Have I ever seemed like I might be the sort of man who would kill a baby?"

"No, of course not." Iggy regarded Myrdin thoughtfully. "So you're Zachary's spy?"

Myrdin nodded. "He doesn't trust Royal Magician Everett."

Iggy drained the last of his soda.

"I suppose I've simply chosen to believe Everett because I've had to. I needed him to break me free of that dog, but if I'm honest I have to admit that his magical preparations don't match his stated goals. And as far as putting a geas on you, I didn't know, Thomas. I always considered you a good friend when we lived in the South Court."

"I didn't think you were part of it. I mean, I knew you were in league with Everett, but I didn't think you would have set me up like that."

A silence settled between them. Myrdin could see Iggy realigning his assessment of their situation.

"I'm curious why you believed that you could be the Guardian of the City. Was that part of the geas?"

"I have dreams." Because he knew Iggy's next request, he went ahead and described them. "I see the city enveloped by fire and screaming."

"Everyone has dreams like that sometimes. Wishful thinking."

"But mine are always the same. I'm protected by a haze of opalescent light, but all around me there's nothing but armies of soulless. They're on fire and still marching."

"But the light protects you?"

"Always. I think I must have read about the light when I was in the Royal Academy of Magic and gotten these ideas. Last week when Everett was here, we talked about it again and he told me he must have been mistaken."

"Well, there's an easy way to check." Iggy stood and brushed the crumbs off his shirt. He took a small transistor radio from a shelf and finding it dead walked to the kitchen to rummage through the drawers, presumably for batteries.

"I've already been tested when I was a boy."

"But who were you tested by? Was it Madame Gantry?"

"I don't remember who tested me. It wasn't Madame Gantry though. I would have remembered her beehive." Myrdin could still vividly picture it.

"Well, if Zachary is right and Everett is attempting to pierce the membrane of the demon realm, then it stands to reason that Everett would have a vested interest in keeping the new guardian untrained or even banned from performing magic, since that child would someday stand in opposition to him. These aren't two-week plans, you know. He's been waiting for these stars to rise since we were in the academy together."

"Why tell me I'm the guardian, though?" Myrdin's hope reignited even as he argued against Iggy.

"To make sure that you felt completely justified in attacking an infant, of course." Iggy finally found a set of batteries and got them situated in the radio's beige plastic housing. He switched the radio on and twisted the dial to the far left. Faintly, Myrdin could hear a series of notes moving in beautiful complexity. He smiled up at Iggy, who searched his face intently. "How many notes do you hear?"

"All of them?" Myrdin answered and Iggy frowned at him in exasperation. "I don't know what you mean."

"Do you hear one noise, or do you hear a song?"

"A song."

"I only hear one note and that note is the most foul, scratching noise I can describe. Only the guardian hears a song."

"I don't remember this being part of the test."

"Then you weren't given the real test. You must have somehow revealed yourself to Everett before the tests even began."

"Then I really am the guardian?"

Iggy nodded. "You most definitely seem to be the rising guardian."

Emotion welled up inside Myrdin, strong enough to bring tears.

"Do you think..." Myrdin fought to keep his voice under control. "Do you think that Everett arranged to have a three-generation ban placed on my line?"

"You mean did he arrange for your parents' prosecution? If what Zachary says is true, then he probably did."

All at once, Myrdin found himself reduced to being a child again, not just in body, but also in his heart. His throat felt hot and his chest tight. Small sobs shook themselves free of his chest and he stood there, fists clenched, powerless to stop them.

"Then my mother and father were killed so that I wouldn't be discovered. It's my fault?" Myrdin asked brokenly.

Iggy knelt before him, hands on Myrdin's arms.

"It's not your fault." Iggy smoothed a hand over Myrdin's hair, then pulled him into his arms. He smelled like aftershave and cinnamon pop. Nothing like Myrdin's own father, yet Myrdin still buried his face in Iggy's neck while Iggy patted his back. "Take a deep breath now. You're all right. It's not your fault."

Myrdin got himself under control soon after, wiping his eyes on his arm and sniffling. Iggy handed him a tissue for his drippy nose.

"This is so undignified."

"I won't tell anybody," Iggy said. "I think you should get your things and get ready to go."

"Where?"

"We should take you to Madame Gantry."

"But I'm a fugitive." Myrdin paused to blow his nose again. "And so are you."

"Madame Gantry has never cared much about the king's laws. And she takes a very liberal view of cheating. Believe me. I used to play pinochle against her and my wife every Friday night. Now get your things. Don't forget your paintbrush."

Myrdin rushed to the small bedroom and gathered the few articles of clothing he'd acquired over the last few days. He felt a pang of loneliness as he folded his three pairs of shorts, two T-shirts and four pairs of socks. He'd grown used to Iggy and his misplaced paternal affection. He didn't know if it was because he had the body of a child now, or whether he'd merely been a child inside all this time, but he found Iggy comforting. Now he was moving again. But at least this time was to the place where he should have been since he was a boy; where he was fated to go from his birth. Everett's spell had managed to reset his life to the exact moment when his first treachery had begun nineteen years ago. If that wasn't fate, what could it be? When he returned to the living room, he found Iggy talking on the phone.

Iggy glanced at Myrdin and said into the phone, "No, Thomas has gone out. Probably buying cigarettes. I told him not to... Yes, Zachary was the same way..." He walked to the window and glanced out through the curtains. "Yes, I see your car. I'll see you soon."

Iggy laid a hand on Myrdin's shoulder to keep him still until the phone call was over. "Everett's here. Listen, I think it would be best if you pretended to be gone. There's a little hole in the wall behind the dryer. Do you think you can get back there?"

Myrdin nodded and Iggy smiled indulgently. "Good. Stay there when Everett arrives. After he's gone we'll get you to Madame Gantry. See, I knew you had greatness in you."

Chapter Nine

Lady Langdon was waiting in the lobby of the Black Tower when Drake returned. Only one man accompanied her and Drake suspected him of being an attorney immediately.

He was not wrong.

"This is Ashton Majender, my notary," Lady Langdon began, once they'd settled themselves in his living room.

"How do you do, sir?" He offered his hand but Ashton refrained from shaking it. Attorneys, especially magical specialists, never shook hands or engaged in any other behavior that could be construed as a binding agreement. They were the weirdest of the court magicians, in Drake's opinion, simultaneously obsessed by the minutiae of spellspeaking and yet unconcerned with the content.

"The pleasure is mine, Grand Magician." Mr. Majender spoke in firm, soft tones. "Lady Langdon has authorized me to offer you the soul of Lord Adam Wexley of the West Court in exchange for your intervention in her granddaughter's possession."

Drake gaped at Majender, then at the old woman.

"I told you before I don't have the expertise to intervene in a possession such as hers."

"Let's just say that I've met enough magicians to know that you're lying."

"He's your godson. How could you offer to sell me his soul?"

"He understands the gravity of our situation," Lady Langdon replied. "He would not object if he knew."

"But you haven't told him your plan, have you?" he asked sourly.

"Nor will I," Lady Langdon said.

Majender cut in quickly. "Wexley's soul is Lady Langdon's to sell, as is the soul of every other courtier in her service. It's a standard contract. Boilerplate."

"Yes, I know. It's only one of the many reasons I am not allied to any court. Surely you understand that I do not accept souls as a form of tender."

"You might not, Grand Magician," Majender spoke as soothingly as he had before, "but there are other magicians who would be more than happy to own Wexley's immortal soul. Lady Langdon would prefer to engage you, though she's willing to find a substitute if necessary."

Understanding came over Drake in one vile wave. She aimed to sell Adam's soul today, if not to him, then to whomever would buy it. Or at least that's what she wanted him to believe. Everett had been right. He'd been too careless around her, given her something to hold over him. The question was would she actually sell Adam's soul if he refused? Probably. Just to spite him.

"You bitch. You extortionist bitch."

Lady Langdon suppressed a laugh. "I'm glad to know that we understand each other, Drake."

"You're supposed to protect him."

"And I will, as best I can. But his first duty is to serve the West Court." Lady Langdon smoothed her neat pencil skirt. "The succession and stability of the kingdom depends on our ability to protect the heir apparent."

"Your granddaughter, you mean?" Drake could not believe she would try to feed him a patriotic line about an action of pure nepotism.

"I would protect any heir no matter which court she came from and I would expect that you, as a patriot, would do the same." Lady Langdon folded her hands in her lap. "Unless you have your own ideas about who should rule."

"You know I care nothing for politics."

"Shall I draw up the contract then?" Majender flipped open the silver latches on his briefcase. The sharp smell of topical anti-infective filled the room. Isopropyl alcohol. Iodine.

Both he and Lady Langdon eyed Drake expectantly.

Despite her brazen display of familial favoritism, Drake suspected Lady Langdon would not frivolously sell her own godson's soul. That must mean that no other grand magician had been able to break the possession. An act of desperation had led her to him. Drake didn't forgive her for her action, but he understood it. He said, "I have two conditions. The first is that no one outside this room will ever know that I own Lord Wexley's soul. Particularly not Lord Wexley. As far as he is concerned, you never betrayed him like this."

"Agreed." Lady Langdon looked relieved. "And the second?"

"I use my own pen."

Majender nodded. Drake withdrew to his office safe to fetch his own blood pen. He thought of filling the cartridge there but knew Majender would demand to witness the bloodletting so he returned and laid out his equipment on the coffee table. Lady Langdon had removed her suit jacket and rolled up the sleeve of her blouse. Majender tied a rubber tourniquet around her biceps. Then he prepared the pen, which looked like a normal fountain pen attached to an intravenous line. Majender inserted the hollow needle into Lady Langdon's arm and had her pump her fist a couple of times while her blood flowed into the cartridge. Then he removed the needle and bandaged her arm.

"May I inspect your instrument, Grand Magician?" he asked and Drake acquiesced, watching carefully to make sure he didn't tamper with it. He opened the casing and looked inside, to ensure that the cartridge was not already loaded with someone else's blood. It was not. Satisfied, he began laying out the contract while Drake inserted his own needle, drew his own blood and bandaged his own arm. The signing of the contract went quickly, which was good for Drake, who felt hot and sick.

"This contract binds you to intervene on behalf of the heir apparent in the matter of possession from this moment until the possession has been broken." Majender handed him a copy, along with the deed to Adam's soul. "We will expect to see you in the West Court by sunrise."

Drake simply nodded his reply, happy to note that Lady Langdon seemed just as ill as he did.

Adam carefully held the feeding bottle to the princess's lips watching without revulsion as she sloppily nursed at the rubber nipple. The girl was a pathetic sight. He couldn't understand how Drake had so little pity for her. She'd just been born and already she was the pawn of her elders.

Lady Carolyn, the princess's mother, stirred and stretched and looked around.

"How is she?"

"Calming down," Adam replied.

"Where are her nurses?" Lady Carolyn searched the room and saw only military medical personnel.

"Royal Magician Everett found spells on all of the nurses. He took them away to purify them."

"And Mother?"

"She said she had an appointment," Adam said. "She'll be back by seven."

Lady Carolyn drew close and Adam relinquished the bottle to her.

"Thank you for looking after her." Lady Carolyn spoke to him but gazed down at the princess, who smiled as her mother's face loomed over the gurney. Baby formula dribbled down the princess's cheek. Lady Carolyn petted the girl's hair. Adam saw her hand tremble and looked to Lady Carolyn's face with concern. Her lip quivered then her face crumpled in a spasm of sorrow.

"Lady Carolyn!" Adam put the bottle aside and went to her, hands on her shoulders. Deprived of her dinner, the princess began to wail. Ear-splitting howls. Adam tried to reinsert the bottle but the princess, fueled by her mother's anxiety, passed the point of consolation. The army medics stood stoically by. Adam felt a convulsive hatred toward them for their heartless reserve.

"I can't bear to see her tied up like a lunatic!" Lady Carolyn choked, her cheeks reddened. Adam observed on her face the visceral sympathy of a mother for her child and did not intervene when she pulled the restraints away even though he knew the king would have objected.

Suddenly free, the princess flailed toward her mother, lurched clumsily sideways and fell off the gurney. Adam dropped to his knees, managing to catch the princess's shoulders as she fell and keep her skull from cracking against the floor. Lady Carolyn collapsed to his side, pulling her daughter into her arms and rocking and whispering to the screaming girl. Finally, when offered a breast, the princess quieted. Adam averted his gaze politely and found the army medics staring on the scene. One with horrified disgust, the other with obvious arousal at what appeared to be one adult woman suckling another. Adam stood.

"Lady Carolyn requires her privacy," he said stiffly. "You are dismissed."

The medics glanced to one another, then to Adam as if to assess Adam's rank before deciding whether or not to comply. One said, "We'll be right outside if you need us, my lord."

Adam gave the medics a curt nod and waited while they left, making sure the door closed behind them. He turned back to Lady Carolyn, still rocking, singing softly to the princess. He dropped into a chair beside the bed, suddenly more tired than he realized. His mind wandered to Drake again, whose sinewy body and soft mouth he'd so recently discovered. Why would Drake go out of his way to help a barista, but not the princess? Did he hate the king as Lord Sapphire had? It didn't follow.

Had Drake refused because Lady Langdon was the one who asked? Though he hadn't known the grand magician long, Adam could still feel the strength of his influence over the other man. If he went alone to the Black Tower and offered himself to Drake, he felt sure that Drake would help the West Court.

Lady Carolyn still sat on the yellow carpet, rocking and singing to her now sleeping daughter. Adam approached them quietly, not wanting to disturb either. He told Lady Carolyn his plan and she nodded in agreement.

"The grand magician has a weakness for you. Mother has spoken of it often of late." Lady Carolyn gave him one of her warm, grateful smiles. The smile that had won the king's heart away from Lord Sapphire. "You have my leave to go."

Though Adam's car passed Lady Langdon's returning limousine on the palace drive neither noticed the other, both being absorbed by thoughts of Drake.

When Adam arrived, Drake expected that he had discovered Lady Langdon's deal and would demand that his soul be returned to him. Instead, he laid his palms lightly on Drake's shoulders. The scarce weight of his hands immobilized Drake as effectively as any binding spell.

"I'm sorry Lady Langdon called you a coward," he said. "I wanted to tell you, but you left too quickly."

"I had other things to do." Drake gave him a tight smile that felt more of a facial tick than an expression. Adam's hand traveled up his shoulder. He rested his palm on the side of his neck and without thinking Drake leaned into it.

"Were you rescuing more souls?" Adam asked.

"In a way."

"Look, I don't understand much about magic, but please tell me honestly, is there really nothing you can do for the princess? Can you not break the possession?" Adam's eyes searched for truth and Drake could not deny him.

"I could break it. But it's complicated."

"If I offered to pay you my soul, would you free her?"

Drake choked, horrified straight to his bones. That Adam would offer his soul for the sake of West Court ambition was awful enough. But the irony that he'd already purchased that same commodity twisted inside Drake. Sickened him. And weak as he was Drake leaned against Adam, his head on Adam's shoulder to hide from Adam's too perceptive eyes. Adam's hand moved to the back of Drake's head and he held him, still with a light touch.

"I am doing my best. You don't have to offer your soul."

"So you're already breaking the spell?" In Adam's voice Drake heard both surprise and pride. His other arm encircled Drake pulling him into a grateful, more substantive embrace. "Of course, you are. I was stupid to think you weren't."

"I must work in my own way." Drake marveled at how much easier speaking to him was when they leaned together like this, when he didn't have to make eye contact. "Please trust me."

"I do trust you... I don't know why, but I do. Is that some kind of spell?"

"If it's a spell, it's one I didn't cast," Drake said. They stood together for a while in the quiet light of afternoon, their bodies remembering how close they'd been the day before. Sleepiness washed over him and he realized he had to stop touching Adam or he'd be too aroused to drive anywhere. "I need to get some caffeine if I'm going to save the princess today."

"Shall I make some?"

"I'll stop at the coffee shop on the way downtown." Drake got his jacket and keys.

"I want to go with you."

"The man I'm going to see doesn't like surprise guests."

Adam hung back. "I don't want to go back to the West Court right now."

"Then stay here. Stay here all night if you like." Drake leaned in quickly and kissed him on the cheek. "The bed misses you anyway."

"Does it really?" Adam smiled and Drake blushed like a virgin.

"I'll return before sundown," he said. "And we'll go to the West Court together."

Adam agreed and they kissed once more and Drake departed.

He drove to his father's place. Police still blockaded his neighborhood, as they had since the seal had broken. Wandering soulless still roamed unchecked down the sidewalks, despite citywide efforts to contain them. There were just too many bodies to accommodate. Both the Royal Stadium and Royal Coliseum were at capacity. Though his own part in the catastrophe had been small, the knowledge that hundreds of people had been severed from their souls edged in on his thoughts, clouding his rationality with corrosive guilt.

Once outside of Tower Heights, fewer soulless perambulated out into the intersections. Drake felt uneasy. At first he pinned his discomfort on the relentless waxing of the Ghost Star, like a red eye winking at him from the horizon, visible now, even in the brightness of the afternoon. But he rejected that, the Ghost Star had pulsed for a week.

No, it was the soulless themselves. Since his father had been made soulless he'd maintained a certain compassion for those empty bodies. Sometimes his emotion even bordered on fondness, never the feeling of suspicion and fear so many of his peers instinctively harbored.

Today, however, they unnerved him. Because the soulless weren't working or even standing motionless and staring as they often did at rest. They moved. They moved in the same direction, not as a mass, but alone or in small clusters, still holding buckets and squeegees or dragging push brooms, all trudging toward the palace.

Only three magicians had the power to move that many bodies simultaneously. His father and Everett were two of them.

The third was Madame Gantry at the museum, but Drake did not imagine that she would summon a soulless army to her side without at least texting him a warning.

Everett planned to strike soon. Maybe even tonight.

He stepped on the gas and tore through the clogged streets with no regard for signals or other drivers, reaching his father's place in less than twenty minutes. The front door hung open. He went in without knocking and was already halfway through the living room before he smelled the sulfur and froze. Some demonic magic had been worked in this place. On his finger, Spider's legs curled inward defensively.

Scanning the room he found a half-finished glass of whiskey, Everett's brand, sitting on the cheap coffee table. Careful not to make a sound, he ran his blood diamond around the rim of the cup and whispered Thomas's name. The boy's image swam to the surface. Dark, huddled behind some machine, shaking.

He lifted Spider to his lips.

"Find him."

Spider let herself down from his hand by a long strand of silk and scrambled through the kitchen. Meanwhile, Drake moved from living room to kitchen to dank bedroom to filthy bathroom, searching.

He hadn't seen Everett's car outside, but that didn't mean he wasn't here. His father's house seemed deserted. He felt a tug on his finger and followed Spider's silk line down the hall to the laundry room. Spider sat atop the dryer, tapping her legs like impatient fingers. The faint noise of metal on metal sounded deafeningly in the quiet. He put out his hand and she climbed back on.

Looking behind the dryer, he initially saw nothing but cobwebs. Then, averting his gaze he saw the top of Thomas's head, bowed over his knees. An easy, but effective spell shielded his small body from direct view.

Leaning down, he whispered, "Where is my father?"

Thomas's eye snapped up to him, relief shining through his tears.

"Downstairs, I think. He told me to hide here when Everett arrived. He said he cast a spell to make me invisible, but you found me."

"I can always find something that belongs to me." Drake kept his voice low. "Is Everett still here?"

"I think he left. I heard him come up the stairs with those filthy birds of his, whistling." Thomas's bottom lip trembled.

"How long ago was that?"

"Only a few minutes. Drake, I..."

"That's Grand Magician Drake to you," Drake said automatically. Growing fear kept him rigid, formal.

Myrdin shrank down and continued, his eyes downcast, his voice barely audible, "Grand Magician, I think Iggy is dead."

Drake could say nothing. In spite of the years he'd spent rehearsing his reaction to this news, he could find no words or emotion, just sickness welling through his stomach and sudden pain wracking his chest.

"We have to get out of here," Thomas pleaded, catching hold of Drake's hand.

But Drake couldn't go. He rushed downstairs into the garage and saw his father there, sprawled on the old couch as if he might have been sleeping. His eyes still and half-open.

"Come on, Grand Magician." Thomas urged from the top of the stairs. "Everett must be stopped!"

"What do you mean?"

"He was trying to get your father to tell him where the Demonslayer sword was hidden. Your father kept denying he'd ever had it but, in the end, I think Iggy confessed everything."

"What did he say?"

"He said the sword was at the museum. That's all I could hear."

Shaking, Drake reached into his father's pockets, searching for his locus or any other magical items, but Everett had left nothing. As he moved his father's heavy limbs Drake became aware of the inert meatiness of the corpse and sickness overcame him. He vomited in the wastebasket.

He dragged a hand across his mouth and reached out to take the worn-out towel Thomas offered him. When had he gone to get that? Drake couldn't remember. He couldn't focus on anything, not even Thomas's insistent begging.

"We have to go." He pulled on Drake's arm. "Please, Grand Magician."

On his finger he felt Spider's legs moving, struggling against the bonds that held her soul. She'd sensed his weakness and began lowering herself from his hand. He caught her and she bit him hard. The pain awakened him and he clamped his fingers harder around her.

"You are not going anywhere, you villain," he growled. She curled her legs inward. Drake felt her capitulation and allowed her to resettle herself on his finger.

He turned to Thomas.

"Where are the souls you and my father trapped?"

"Everett took them with him, or the birds did, anyway." Thomas cast a glance at Drake's father then took a wadded fleece blanket and covered his body while silent tears streamed down his face. Seeing those tears somehow prevented Drake's from emerging. He took Thomas by the shoulder.

"We can't just leave him here. Someone will steal his body." He activated his phone to dial a secure morgue and doing so he found he had messages. The first was from Adam, saying that Madame Gantry had been phoning his apartment and that he'd gone to the museum at her request. The second message was from his father. He hit a key and his father's voice spilled out of the receiver.

"Listen, Zachary. Everett is on his way here and I'm worried that he won't take my withdrawal well. You need to know that the Demonslayer sword is hidden in the museum inside the great leviathan. If Everett goes through with his plan, you'll need it. If not, I suppose I'll see you later. I love you. Goodbye."

And that was all.

The museum—where Adam had gone, where Everett was heading. Drake tried phoning Adam. No answer.

"Please, Grand Magician, we can't stay here. What if Everett comes back?"

"What will we do with the body? I don't want scalpers to reanimate him." Drake stared at Thomas, too overwhelmed to conjure his own answers.

"We'll take it with us."

Drake and Thomas lugged Iggy up the stairs and out onto the quiet street. They settled him in the trunk, respectfully tucked under a blanket. The Ghost Star burned on the horizon like a vile eye glaring down on them. The streets were emptier than they had been, the few cars that shared the street mainly government vehicles, heading uptown. Martial curfew certainly did manage to cut the street congestion.

As he drove, Drake noticed the sky gradually darkening as a black form fell across the sun, plunging the afternoon into a hot and murky twilight. No eclipse should have darkened the sky at this time. It could only be the conjunction of the planes: the demon realm coming close enough to their own to cast its darkness onto their sun. The shadow eclipse had begun and Everett's plan would begin with it.

Hatred more intense than any love or happiness Drake had ever felt flowed through Drake, pulsing through his blood, congealing into an evil rage that filled his heart. Beside him, Thomas sniffled and smoked. After a while Thomas spoke.

"I really liked your dad, even when he lived inside a dog."

"Don't talk about him." Drake's breath caught in his throat. So long as he didn't think of his father, just kept driving, he would be able to do what he had to do. Stop Everett.

Chapter Ten

Despite the curfew, bodies clogged the Tower Heights streets.

Soulless. All going the same direction. Adam could sense Karl's increasing agitation as he wove through their plodding, pedestrian ranks. The sudden eclipse had been hard enough on him, causing all the fur on his back to stand up.

The orangutan laid on the horn, then adjusted his cap and growled. He glanced back in the rearview mirror at Adam, who gave him an apologetic smile.

"After this I'll give you three days off, I swear," Adam said. "I'll buy you that trapeze you want."

His driver nodded and proceeded slowly, honking and nudging between thick clots of soulless. He had a terrible feeling that the sun going out and the massing soulless were related events. And if that was true, his being out among them with *The Book of Demons* could not be safe. But it certainly must be important.

The book in Adam's lap seemed alive. More alive than it had when he'd retrieved it from Drake's bedroom. Even wrapped in Adam's leather jacket, it radiated the heat of a living body. Red lightning crackled across the dark sky and a fat soulless woman lurched out into the path of the car. Karl slammed on the breaks. Adam fell forward but didn't lose his grip on the tome.

A matter of life or death, Madame Gantry had said. Bring the book, she'd said. He'd tried to call Drake but had been unable to connect.

A soulless walking nearby hit Adam's door with a heavy thud. Looking up in alarm, Adam saw the young man's face pressed against the glass. Though his mouth hung slack, his eyes scanned the interior of the car with unusual intelligence. Adam met the soulless man's gaze just as the light of intelligence winked out.

The car inched forward, toward the police checkpoint that had so challenged Adam on his earlier trip to the museum. The police cars had been pushed aside so that they stood askew on the sidewalk. Streetlights shone down on blinking piles of white and orange barricades that lay strewn in the center of the street. Adam could see no police, or even any hint of a blue uniform among the people who clogged the route. Alarm prickled at his skin.

Catching his eye in the rearview mirror, Karl raised a hand to sign, "This doesn't look good, boss," with his thick, dark fingers.

"Keep going." Adam kept his voice calm. Karl did as instructed, gliding by the disrupted barricade. Through the crowd of bodies, Adam thought he glimpsed a police officer, lying on the ground.

Another thud as another soulless jumped on the hood of the car, peering in through the windshield. The man's hands left wet, red marks on the glass. Karl pounded the steering wheel in simian frustration, screaming out animal obscenities, waving his long arms. The museum's colonnade loomed ahead of them. Behind them the soulless had closed ranks, some pushing right up against the back bumper of the car.

Karl signed, "This is fucked up, boss."

"I know. Keep going."

A large, white cockatoo landed on the hood beside the soulless man, cocked its head and fixed Adam with one eye. Another bird alighted and then a third, all watching Adam. Sorcerer's familiars, there could be no doubt. The birds cawed and squawked and the soulless, who had merely been walking alongside, converged on the car. Adam lunged forward and locked the passenger-side door just as an old woman began to lift the handle.

They were looking at the book, he realized. Somehow someone was controlling these soulless.

Adam grabbed Karl's hairy shoulder.

"We've got to get inside that building, I don't care how we do it!"

Outside a soulless man pulled a branch from an ornamental cherry tree and started beating the window. Karl stepped on the gas. The birds flew aside and the windshield cracked as the big soulless man slammed into it. Karl gunned it, driving up onto the colonnade thick with bodies. Karl swerved, trying to avoid them, but the soulless put themselves in front of the car. Not quickly, just deliberately like pawns moving themselves out on a chessboard. Adam flinched as another body hit the windshield with a sickening, bloody thump. The cracked glass crumpled inward. Immediately another soulless, a woman in overalls jumped onto the hood and shoved her hands through the broken windshield, pulling away the glass.

They were only yards from the museum now, but between them and the massive pentagrammed doors lay a sea of flesh.

Karl plowed into the crowd screaming and honking as he drove over them, the car bumped over their broken limbs and still they made no sound, no expression. When the dented and bloody grill of Adam's car rested against the wooden doors, Karl hit the brakes. Soulless pressed in on every side. Now that the car had stopped, Adam could hear the birds screeching, cawing, whistling. The air was alive with the sounds of birds. Three parrots dove in through the hole in the windshield to attack Karl.

Adam lunged forward, beating at the birds.

Then the museum doors opened.

Opalescent light poured out around the statuesque figure of Madame Gantry. With one raised hand, she sent a blast of wind hurtling at the soulless who scattered and fell off Adam's car.

"Get inside!" she bellowed. "Both of you!"

The orangutan needed no encouragement. He leapt through the broken windshield, turned and hauled Adam through with one long, strong arm. The wind kept surging up, blasting any body that strayed too close. Adam stumbled into the museum's lobby behind Karl bloody and shaking. The doors closed behind them.

Madame Gantry spun on them, eyes wild.

"Did you bring it?"

Adam straightened up and gave a low, formal bow.

"Your book, Madame Gantry."

As she took the book, her face lit in beatific relief.

"You have my eternal gratitude, Lord Wexley," Madame Gantry said. Then, turning to Karl, "And you have my thanks as well, sir."

Karl shrugged and actually looked bashful. Madame Gantry turned back to Adam. "I must hurry. Everett has nearly arrived."

"What can I do?"

Madame Gantry seemed suddenly sad. She laid a hand on his shoulder. "You've done all you can, Lord Wexley. I suggest you hide. Everett will be looking for me and for the book upstairs. If you go to the basement there is a cafeteria. Stay there, he'll pass right over you." Madame Gantry looked thoughtful then added, "And the vending machines should keep you adequately fed. I will come for you when the fight is over."

"I want to help you!"

Madame Gantry shook her head. "You cannot. Now go."

Karl already tugged on Adam's arm, pointing at the clearly marked staircase with its sign reading *Refreshments*.

"Madame, I am a gentleman and I will not leave you behind." Adam lifted his chin, his stance firm. Behind him, Karl let out a howl of simian frustration.

"If that's the case, you can do one thing for me. I must erect a barrier around the city to restrain Everett's movements. I cannot be interrupted. Don't let him up these stairs until my incantations are complete."

"How will I know when you're finished?"

"I will send a sign." Madame Gantry bounded up the big staircase with spry haste Adam hadn't expected from such an old woman. Adam turned to Karl.

"You don't have to stay with me."

Karl shrugged and shook his head. He gave Adam a forced grin and thumbs up.

"Thank you." As he spoke, Adam felt the concussive shudder of something massive pounding against the doors. The big doors bowed inward. Adam rushed back through the lobby, searching for anything to block the doors. Then he caught sight of the big diorama of King Simon slaying the leviathan. He jumped into the diorama, seized the Demonslayer sword and pulled. The sword, and King Simon's entire arm, came away. Papier mache and wax and foil. Surrounded by fake weapons, Adam's spirits sank. Here were the Lance of Mortimer, the Demonslayer sword, the Horn of Souls. And, of course, *The Book of Demons*, or a faux suede replica of it.

The pounding continued, relentless. Adam heard a crack and saw a flash of flame spew inward. Fear gripped him and he renewed his search for anything of use. The floor shook. Foam rocks crumpled under his weight. The replica *Book of Demons* fell.

Another crack and the museum's front door exploded inward in a barrage of planks and splinters. Soulless streamed in. Adam steeled himself for an onslaught, but they didn't even look his way. The whole procession filed past him, toward the exhibits.

Karl pulled him down behind the fallen statue of King Simon. Adam almost struggled then saw the wisdom in this. Obviously, Everett didn't know Madame Gantry's location. Better to let him wander the wrong direction than call attention to their presence. Maybe they could find a real weapon to fight with or, failing that, a sturdy fake.

The long column of soulless shuffled wordlessly inside.

Among them, like a rock star cocooned within his entourage, came the Royal Magician Everett. Tropical birds swooped and wheeled in the air above him. He whistled to himself as he walked into the Hall of Ancient Bones.

Adam glanced to Karl then quietly crept after them, moving slowly at the tail end of the crowd. The soulless were in

Everett's thrall completely. They looked where he looked, surrounding him in a wall of compliant insulating flesh.

When Everett reached the massive articulated skeleton of the great leviathan, he stepped over the red velvet rope surrounding the exhibit and walked beneath the skeleton, turned and helped a young woman step clumsily over the barrier. Adam's eyes widened in horror as he recognized Princess Julianna. Though every fiber of his being wanted to rush forward and rescue her, Adam restrained himself. Madame Gantry worked to save the city and everyone in it. The princess, no matter how important, was only one person.

Everett held a pocket watch in his left hand. He held his right hand up and out as if conducting a symphony. The princess moved forward.

Reaching up into the skeleton, she grabbed one protruding spur of bone and pulled. The bone came down and down, lengthening, revealing the blade of an unmistakable sword. The Demonslayer. The princess swayed, moving in jerky marionette-like movements. Adam could hear Everett's quiet voice.

"True blood of kings awaken, Demonslayer!" At his words, the princess gripped the sword hard. The old bone colored instantly, drawing blood out of her and turning crimson. She paled and swayed, but stayed standing.

Everett looked up through the glass dome above and all the soulless followed his gaze. Even Adam looked up to where the Ghost Star pulsed high in the sky.

Everett snapped his pocket watch shut and the click resounded through the still building.

From his pocket he took an old utility knife. He unfolded a small blade and held the edge up to the sky. He made what looked like a small slash through the air, and the air parted like a cut opening. Tiny at first, the cut seeped wind and yellow sparks as it ripped wide, growing from the size of a hand to a gaping chasm as high as the leviathan. Hot, acrid wind blew out and the air filled with the sound of screeching.

A puncture between the realms! Adam drew in breath and flinched back from the sound. In the old songs, they spoke of a wound in the air opening to the demon world and the terrible creatures beyond.

The soulless remained impassive. Even the ones closest to Everett who were showered with sparks stood like statues, their skin reddening. Four of them began to unravel a net as vast as a parachute and so fine that it was nearly invisible. Everett's attention remained on the other side of the rift.

"Come on, my beauty," Everett cooed. He reached into his pocket and held up a stone. "Come here, my sweet."

Through the door came a bird's head made entirely of fire. A phoenix.

Everett extended his hand to the princess. She handed him her sword as the phoenix continued to struggle, pulling her long wings through the rift between the realms.

When Everett had coaxed her forward, the soulless moved, hurling the net over her. She screamed and struggled. Searing pain shot through Adam's ears, then two pops and he heard nothing more. Looking beside him, he saw Karl clutching the sides of his head. Blood seeped down from the princess's ears.

Everett motioned again and the rift between the realms closed. Everett approached the thrashing phoenix and rested the tip of the Demonslayer against the phoenix's breast.

In the silence of deafness, Adam felt as though he were in a dream. The words of an old ballad floated through his mind. King Simon pierced the traitor's breast and Demonslayer sent his soul away.

At the lightest touch of the blade, even on its vaporous body, the phoenix went limp. Her head fell down like a servant undergoing the ritual of severance. At once, Adam understood.

The Demonslayer could sever the connection between body and soul. So now the phoenix's body lay momentarily helpless and Adam with horror realized what would happen next. Everett planned to possess the phoenix—to put his own soul inside the monster.

Everett made a gesture, then his body went slack like any of the other soulless. The phoenix twitched. Its massive, fiery wings flopped down. This was the moment that Everett's soul was moving to the body of the phoenix.

Adam saw, with sudden clarity, that he had an opportunity to stop Everett.

He ran forward, shoving his way through inert soulless. He reached the princess just as the phoenix began to revive. Snatching the Demonslayer from Everett's own lax grip, Adam plunged it into Everett's chest. Blood sprayed out like a geyser. Everett's body crumpled forward, a sad, shocked, stupid expression on his face. Adam jerked the blade out of Everett and thrust again. The old man's mouth moved as his blood sprayed up, but Adam could see that he had been too late. Everett's soul had already been transferred into the phoenix. Adam had only managed to kill Everett's soulless body.

A blast of scorching wind brought his attention to Everett's new body awakening. The phoenix's wings flapped once. Its head came up and, seeing Everett's body lying on the floor, craned over to nudge his dying form.

Adam ran. Demonslayer in hand, hacking at the soulless who grasped at him in the stifling, eerie silence. He felt the phoenix scream again, vibrating through his guts like rolling thunder.

He couldn't outrun a phoenix, but he had to run as hard as he could to keep Madame Gantry safe as long as possible.

Rushing through the lobby, he seized the replica *Book of Demons*, turned and ran for it. He didn't look back. He didn't need to. He could feel the phoenix literally hot on his heels.

He turned left into a stairwell. He leapt up the stairs two at a time while the phoenix's head crashed through the door behind him. Over his shoulder he saw the phoenix's mouth open and felt the shockwave of its scream. He rushed up to the mezzanine overlooking the lobby and dove beneath a display table, scrambling across the carpet tiles. Soulless pressed in all around him, grabbing his ankle, his arm. The phoenix bashed its head down the narrow hall, trying to catch him.

This was the end. His last stand.

Eerie calm passed through him, and he thought that he should die standing up, like the noble lord he was. He pushed himself to his feet and held the fake *Book of Demons* aloft.

"Royal Magician!" Though Adam could not hear his own voice, he shouted with all of his force. Sweat trickled down into this face, stinging his eyes. "Stop or I'll use this!"

The phoenix cocked its head at him, peering at the book.

Adam pulled the book open and bellowed out the words he remembered Drake reading, "To Hell's heart I command you go! With my words—"

A cockatoo swooped down at Adam. He slammed his hand into it, bringing it down before it could get too close a look at the book.

The phoenix loomed over him.

Then sudden cold cut through the haze of heat. Black bands of frigid shadow wrapped around his body holding him motionless. Fear surged through him, but as he stared around he saw all the soulless frozen like he was, wrapped in these same bonds. The phoenix turned and flew down from the mezzanine. Adam struggled against the black bonds and they tightened. Sickening happiness emanated from them as if the bonds themselves wanted him to struggle, loved holding him helpless there. Fear like nothing he'd ever felt gripped Adam. Drake rushed into view, lips moving, and expression tense.

He pressed his claw ring into one of the bonds holding Adam and the oily blackness retreated from his limbs back into the ring.

"Madame Gantry!" Adam said as soon as he was able. Drake flinched putting a hand to his ear. Adam modulated his voice instantly. "I'm sorry if I'm yelling," he whispered. "I can't hear. Drake, I think I killed Royal Magician Everett—not his soul, but his body."

Drake looked worried and gave Adam's hand a reassuring squeeze. A boy rushed up beside Drake, face flushed and talking fast.

Drake pulled Adam to him, his hands shaking a little where they rested against Adam's back. He felt the magician's breathing quicken, become uneven and then calm. The boy looked on, a sad, passive expression on his face and Adam realized he knew him.

"Lord Sapphire," he said. The boy nodded and spoke, gesturing wildly.

Behind young Lord Sapphire, the lobby was still, bound bodies of soulless scattering the floor, the mezzanine stairwell and the hallway leading to the dioramas. No sign of the phoenix, though. Through the cracked main doorway, Adam saw police cars gathering on the colonnade, their red and blue lights flashing. Uniformed officers approached, guns drawn.

Adam pulled back and smoothed Drake's hair back from his face. The magician's eyes looked tired, his face drawn with tension and sadness. He wanted to ask what had happened, but knew he wouldn't be able to hear the answer anyway.

"Royal Magician Everett has put his soul into the body of a phoenix." Adam offered Drake the sword. "He did it with this sword."

Drake pushed the sword back. He lifted a hand and signed, "Keep it for now."

Madame Gantry's spell was only half-powered. Drake could see that as soon as he crossed the threshold into her sanctum. She'd poured a wide circle of salt around the Royal District including the Tower Heights and Flower Market neighborhoods. Thin smoke rose up from the circle, creating a faint dome. If the spell had been fully powered, he wouldn't have been able to see through it, but now the smoke swirled and scattered, Madame Gantry's spell being dismantled. Probably by Everett's birds.

Madame Gantry clutched the edge of her table, staring fiercely at the dome, visibly willing it to existence. Sweat rolled down her cheeks dampening her fine, gray hair.

"I'm attempting to contain Everett's influence within this area and slowly draw the circle tighter to keep him corralled above the palace grounds."

"Why the palace?"

"It's the least populated, best protected part of the city." She dabbed at her brow with a hanky. "This is very strenuous for a woman at my stage of life."

"I can see that." Drake scanned the tiny city before him. "Adam said that Everett has inhabited a phoenix."

"How is Lord Wexley?" Madame Gantry's tone remained light.

"Deaf, but otherwise unharmed. His chauffeur is looking after him. He's managed to recapture the Demonslayer from Everett."

Madame Gantry gave a rueful smile. "I guess he was right about being able to be of use."

Thomas burst through the door at that moment, face flushed with elation.

"Everett's body is among the slain!" he announced, his childish enthusiasm evident. He stopped, eyes roving between Madame Gantry and Drake, searching for an enthusiastic response that wasn't there. "That's good, isn't it?"

"Yes and no. Killing Everett's body has removed his escape route," Drake said.

"If Everett feels trapped he will lash out more violently," Madame Gantry explained to Thomas. She used a soft tone, as if he really was the child he appeared to be. Thomas bit his lip and gazed at his shoes. Madame Gantry laid her papery hand on the back of his neck. "Don't worry. We will protect you..."

"Thomas," Drake supplied. "And he's not as young as he seems."

Thomas responded to her, leaning in to her touch, hungry as a dog that no one has petted in a long time. The thought of dogs brought him back to his father, lying waxy in his trunk, and he turned his attention immediately to the model. The protective dome Madame Gantry hoped to construct shredded before their eyes. Madame Gantry slumped, as if physically punched, into Thomas, who struggled to hold her up.

Immediately, Drake crossed the table to help steady her. She caught her breath, straightened and pushed them both away.

"Drake, I need someone to help me with this shield."

"Let me do it." Thomas gazed up at Madame Gantry's gaunt face. "You only need someone to feed you energy, correct? I learned that in school."

"In the academy?" Madame Gantry asked.

"Yes, it was a long time ago, but I still know the basics." Thomas seemed to belatedly remember that he was Drake's property. But rather than asking for permission he smiled a strange, smug smile and stepped up before Madame Gantry, raising his chin proudly. "Anyway it's my duty because I'm the next guardian."

Both he and Madame Gantry stared at Thomas, startled by his announcement. Hope welled up inside him and he could see this same desire light Madame Gantry's haggard face. If that was true, they had a real chance at winning; he had some hope of avenging his father's murder. Then familiar skepticism rolled up to quash his nascent hope almost immediately.

"Did Everett tell you that?" Drake asked. He felt sorry for Thomas, still under the delusions that Everett had induced in his broken heart.

"No, Iggy did," he told Drake. He moved closer to Madam Gantry. "I can hear the star's music."

"Can you?" She bent to look into Myrdin's eyes as if she could read the truth there. And maybe she could. Drake watched her, desperate for her to accept Thomas's claim.

"We'll soon see if you're correct, Thomas."

Outside the shrieks of the phoenix ripped through the air. He had no luxury to wait to see the outcome of their experiment, knowing that he must face Everett regardless.

Drake bowed to Madame Gantry. "You may use Thomas as you see fit but not past the extent of his desire. Until my return, I leave the protection of his soul to you."

Madame Gantry laughed, but sadness tinged her voice as she realized that he had just formally willed possession of Thomas's soul to her and what that implied about his hopes for the future.

"You speak as a true grand magician, Drake. If you must go, take Lord Wexley with you. He has a knack for being helpful."

Drake heard, but had no intention of complying. If he could leave Adam here in her care, it would be best. He loped down the stairs two at a time and raced through the colonnade to his car, where Adam waited, waving from the passenger seat. The Demonslayer lay across his lap.

"Bolt the door."

Myrdin did as he was instructed. As he pushed the deadbolts into place, he could suddenly feel the energy in the room, like the act of sliding the deadbolt home completed a magical circuit. The sound of the phoenix flying overhead faded beneath the heartbreaking notes and harmonies that were the music of the Guardian Star.

"It's so beautiful," Myrdin whispered.

Madame Gantry nodded, and motioned him to her side. "Do you have your locus?"

Myrdin nodded. Delving into his pocket, he produced the paintbrush. The slim wooden handle had been broken in half during the fracas below with Everett's soulless army, but the brush itself was still intact. He smoothed the bristles down into a fine point. He could almost see the wisps of power coming off the brush's tip as he groomed it.

"Focus on the light within you and push it through the locus, just as you learned in school." Madame Gantry's face remained calm, though her voice was strained. "I need you to—"

Madame Gantry's instructions were cut short. Her body rocked forward as if she'd been struck by a massive, invisible force. She held out her hand to Myrdin. He clasped her damp, cold fingers, trying to channel the light within himself into her.

"No." Madame Gantry shook her head. Blood ran from both nostrils. "I am not strong enough now to build the shield around the city. You'll have to do that without me."

"But I don't know how!"

"Use your locus to draw a ring around this model, where the salt is. The spell is already set, it just needs something to power it." One of Madame Gantry's long, gray locks came loose from its confinement of hairspray and hung next to her face. "Everett's kept you hidden from me all this time because he knew he couldn't oppose two guardians at once. Just let him keep throwing himself at me and he'll be too busy to notice your work. *Now do it.*"

Myrdin gulped as the weight of his task settled on his shoulders. His hand looked so small as he lifted his brush. But he focused inside, on the Guardian Star's music, on her opalescent light. The sounds of soulless moaning at the door diminished to a hum. He channeled his energy on the brush in his hand and drew a circle around the city, watching in awe as Madame Gantry's diorama instantly lit. The wispy smoke of the dome coalesced into a hard haze of light. Inside he could still see the bright shape of the phoenix moving, searching for a weakness. He felt the phoenix throw itself at the barrier. He saw the impact as Madame Gantry convulsed forward as if hit with a massive hammer.

Rage welled up within him like a geyser and Myrdin poured it into the dome holding the phoenix inside. From above, Myrdin could hear the faraway screams of the phoenix. More and more light flowed into him and Myrdin felt himself burning inside, trying to control it.

"Don't hold back." Madame Gantry's hollow voice penetrated the morass of his thoughts. "Give yourself to the star."

"No, it's too much!"

Though her face was gaunt and wrinkled, her eyes sparkled like those of a little girl. She smiled at him, placed her hand on his. Her skin was thin and dry as tissue paper and nearly transparent against his plump child's hand.

"Don't be afraid."

Myrdin gave himself to the star and light flooded through him. It burned away his rage, his sadness, his emptiness. Even his memory seemed distant, like something that he'd once read, but didn't belong to him. He saw that same light coursing through Madame Gantry. He smiled at her. They were together now. Chosen by the same distant star.

"Now," she said. "Let's catch that bird."

Adam didn't do anything but hold on as Drake drove, like a mad orangutan, through the crowded streets. He crashed through a police barricade, barely avoiding the soulless who still shuffled through the streets, massing toward the palace. Adam kept his hand gripped around the hilt of the Demonslayer.

Holding it felt good, as if it was his fate. He only wished his ears would clear up. He raised a hand to his ear and drew it back, seeing the blood on his fingers, and knew his deafness wasn't temporary. He looked to Drake. The magician stared straight ahead. Focused on the road, rage and sorrow played undisguised across his face.

Adam wasn't the only person who had lost something today, he realized. Chaos reigned. The closer they came to the palace grounds, the more buildings were on fire. Walls of heat penetrated the open car window. Drake flinched, slammed on the breaks and clamped his hands over his ears. The car skidded to a halt. Drake kept his hands clutched over his ears. Adam took this opportunity to take the keys. Drake didn't notice. When he finally removed his hands, tears streamed down his cheeks.

"Are you all right?" Adam asked.

Drake answered. One or two words. Adam couldn't tell if he'd said yes or no. He suspected the grand magician said something like "I'm fine," which was clearly untrue. Drake felt for the keys and, finding them gone, started frantically searching the floor. When he couldn't find them there, Drake banged his hands on the steering wheel screaming out his rage, his face contorted. On Drake's hand, Adam could see Spider's legs starting to move as she tried to pull herself away.

"You need to focus, Drake," Adam said. The vibration in his throat was the only thing that reassured him he was speaking at all. He laid a hand atop Spider, whose twitching legs unnerved him. Drake glanced over and seemed to notice Adam for the first time. He noticed the keys in Adam's hand specifically. "Your ring's trying to escape again. Did something happen?"

Drake tried to pull his hand from beneath Adam's, but Adam didn't allow it. Tears dripped down Drake's cheeks. He raised his free hand and signed, "Everett killed my father."

"I'm sorry." Adam gave Drake's hand a squeeze. Spider stopped twitching.

Drake signed again, "I'm going to kill Everett tonight."

"I'll help you."

Drake shook his head. "Get out of the car."

"No, I'm going with you."

"Not while I own you. Now hand over those keys and get out."

Adam felt the impact of Drake's spell immediately. His muscles moved, responding to Drake's command. The grand magician really did own him. Sickness and shock flowed over him to realize that Lady Langdon had sold him. He struggled to keep Drake's car keys in his hand but could only watch himself placing them in Drake's palm.

"You can control my body, but you can't make me stop wanting to fight beside you."

"No, but I can stop you from going."

"Please Drake. Don't take this chance from me. Don't leave me behind."

"Chance for what?" Drake's lips moved along with his hands.

"A place in history!" Adam shouted. He could feel the strain of it in his throat.

"You already killed his body. Can't that be enough history for you?" Drake covered his face with his hands.

"I want to be there with you when you win." Again Adam struggled to free himself of Drake's thrall and found himself once more in control of his body. Drake had released him.

Adam pried his hands away, leaned forward and kissed Drake's forehead.

"You will win, Drake. You are the greatest magician alive."

Drake lurched forward into Adam's shoulder, wrapping his hard arms around Adam, holding him so tight that it hurt. He felt Drake draw in a shuddering breath, felt his fingers clutching the back of Adam's shirt. He pulled away and scrubbed a hand across his face.

He signed, "If you can get close enough, this sword will separate the royal magician's soul from the phoenix. Once her body is free of Everett's control, the phoenix will be able to reunite with her own soul and will return to the demon realm on her own."

"Are you sure?"

Drake nodded, signing, "It's in her nature to want to go home."

"I can do that. Now give me back the keys, I'm driving." Adam smoothed Drake's hair back from his face. "Because at the rate you're going, you'll kill us both before we even get to the palace."

Drake relented and Adam seated himself in the driver's seat. He eased Drake's car out into the chaos of the street, weaving around soulless, emergency vehicles and wrecked cars. Already fires engulfed whole buildings where the phoenix had alighted. The pavement smelled hot.

Looking up, Adam saw the phoenix fly overhead toward the palace. Drake clutched his head in agony. Soulless and policemen on the street fell, twitching, to the ground.

"He's gone to the palace." Adam could feel himself shouting, though he could not hear the words.

Drake nodded at him and Adam hit the gas.

Once through the south gate, Adam could see the phoenix clearly, perched on the front steps of the palace, flapping its fiery wings. He turned onto the lawn, driving through the corridor Drake had blasted the night the Medallion of Amabel had been cracked. He stopped the car at the base of the statue of Queen Rexella.

Outside the car, the wind whipped around like heat from a blast furnace. The phoenix seemed to consume the entire sky. Beads of sweat sprang up on Adam's brow. From all directions, squadrons of soldiers advanced on the palace only to be consumed by geysers of flame belched by the phoenix. A battery of fire trucks sat near the palace steps, some burning, some still functioning, blasting water at the phoenix and at the burning palace roof.

"Are you ready?" Adam asked, hefting the sword in his hand.

Drake nodded. He said something and Adam shook his head. "I don't understand."

Drake grabbed Adam's jaw and pressed a kiss onto his mouth. Adam returned it gladly, smiling. Then Drake started down the short path toward the palace.

All around them, soldiers lay scattered like dolls. Some lay dead, others were merely soulless, shuddering and empty. Drake kept his eye on them, knowing that Everett could, at any moment, possess them all.

Beside him, Adam seemed to be focusing on the blazing shape of the phoenix atop the palace roof, beating its wings and casting jumping shadows over the apocalyptic landscape that used to be the royal labyrinth. Adam looked as handsome and noble as a figure in a tapestry. That he would face death so well made Drake's heart ache with pride.

A veil of thick black smoke wafted across his face and he smelled searing metal. The phoenix scanned the ground, its eyes of blue flame, searching for opponents. And then the flame blue gaze settled on Drake and the phoenix—as Everett—cocked his head in recognition.

It leapt into the air and alighted before them, wilting the grass in a wide circle around it. Everett remained wary of the Demonslayer and stayed out of Adam's reach.

"Drake." Everett's voice, though filtered through a throat of hollowed flame, was unmistakable. "Whatever you're thinking of doing, it's futile. Today begins the reign of a new regime."

"Yours?"

"Of course, mine," Everett hissed. "It could be yours as well. I understand your confusion. Your father and I should have told you what we were doing."

At the mention of his father, Drake's hands began to tremble with rage.

"You didn't have to kill him!" Drake's words felt like they had been ripped out of his throat. "You could have let him go!"

"So you know." A note of remorse colored Everett's voice. "I'm sorry, Drake. I had hoped you wouldn't find out about the differences between us."

"You fucking bastard! How can you—" Drake broke off, his voice cracking with rage. He had not come here to argue with Everett about the validity of his domination plan. He came for retribution.

"Drake." The phoenix ventured slightly closer. Adam lunged forward, sword high, driving him back. "There is still hope for you. You don't have to die like this, pointlessly defending a king who dislikes you. I'll even let your plaything live, though I must say I'm rather irritated at him at the moment. Just give me the sword and join me."

"Never," Drake said.

"Suit yourself." The phoenix reared up and Adam slashed at the flames. Everett leapt back and drew in a massive breath. Drake felt severing magic moving through the air. Beside him Adam convulsed, choking. Drake felt his own soul move inside his body and focused tightly down, clenching his teeth, forcing himself to remain integrated.

A strangled cry erupted from Adam as his soul was pulled from his body. The phoenix opened its mouth. All around souls flew toward it. The phoenix breathed them in like smoke, eating their power.

Drake staggered forward, reaching Adam's body just as it fell forward onto its hands and knees. Bereft of memory, intellect and hearing, Adam's body dropped the Demonslayer and hunched like an animal on the grass, whimpering.

Everett launched himself into the air away from the Demonslayer and outside the range of Drake's most intense power. He circled high in the air. The soulless around him began to stir. As one, they turned their dull eyes on Drake. So many of them. But many too grossly wounded that their progress was slow. One palace guard lurched toward him, intestines slopping out of a wound in his side. Another's face had been burnt beyond recognition. Drake knew it would only be a matter of time before they ripped him apart. Even Adam looked up at him with that same torpid malevolence. Drake jammed Talon into Adam's neck. He had to keep Adam's body safe long enough to get his soul back inside, and in this chaos, it would be easy to get separated.

"Protect him," he told Spider. She dropped from Drake's hand and began to build a web in the air, to shelter Adam's body. Drake closed his hand around the hilt of the Demonslayer sword. It felt lighter than he expected.

He focused his power and let a concussive burst out all around him. The soulless within twenty feet fell crippled beneath it. Outrage filled Drake. His hate and betrayal galvanized into one singular desire to get Adam's soul back. It belonged to him and he had never lost hold of what was his.

Everett wheeled in the air, soaring up and out toward the edge of the city. Then he suddenly turned and Drake saw him fly a tight circle just outside the palace grounds. Everett's next pass was even tighter as if his flight was being slowly constricted.

It had to be Madame Gantry's magical barrier. Thomas must have had enough power to help her fuel it. Hope glimmered up in Drake's chest. He had the chance he needed.

Everett slammed against it, sending flames pouring up, showing the dimensions of the invisible dome that held him prisoner. Drake realized Everett would attempt to return to the museum to kill Madame Gantry and free himself. When he did so, his flight path would bring him directly overhead.

Drake concentrated on Adam's soul, whispering his name over the blood diamond until he could see the hot thread of light stretching between Drake and the phoenix. Adam's soul lay deep inside Everett, twisting and lurching, still fighting.

Pride surged up inside Drake as he watched Adam struggle, even though he had no body, no power against the demonic form that Everett inhabited.

Spider's net was nearly complete. Adam's deaf and soulless body lay curled in a ball on the ground. Drake thought it was crying. He stared up into the sky, watching Everett's wings beat and the flames roll out along the invisible dome, making the sky seem to boil.

Drake wrapped his finger around the thread between himself and Adam willing his strength into it. He leaned close and whispered, "I take back what is mine."

Light glinted along the thread.

Everett passed directly over and Drake pulled with all his might. Hand over hand he reeled Adam's soul through the phoenix's body. The phoenix lurched in the air beating its wings reflexively up. Drake could see Everett trying to control the demon's nature, make her fly down toward Drake instead of away, but he could not make her stop struggling upward for freedom.

Drake held firm, yanking the thread farther down until the phoenix's flaming body was within reach. Sweat ran down his face, he smelled his hair scorching. Then with one stroke Drake raised the Demonslayer and slashed her belly open. Hundreds of souls exploded from the fiery confines, writhing like smoke from the wound.

From amid smoke, Drake pulled Adam's soul free. The phoenix shot back into the sky, thrashing in the air like a fish on the floor of a boat, finally crashing down to earth, igniting the North Court in an explosion of sparks.

The soulless surrounding Drake stilled, all wounded now and cowering, rocking themselves, crying.

Drake held Adam's fragile soul in his cupped palms. Lifting his hands to his lips, Drake breathed Adam's soul in, holding it inside his mouth for safekeeping. He had to get out of here, get Adam someplace safe.

A scream split the sky and Drake looked sharply up.

In the distance he could see the phoenix bend and with her teeth pull the long black ribbon of Everett's soul from the wound. She jerked it out of her belly and flung it across the palace grounds, then staggered to her feet.

Her wound closed up and she flapped her wings and stamped the earth, sending a thunderous tremor across the grounds. The statue of Queen Rexella toppled from its pedestal, smashing to pieces on the ground.

The black ribbon coalesced in midair and dived down, searching for an empty body, but the phoenix was faster. She wheeled and chased, breathing swathes of blue fire across the night sky. Flames ignited the trees and the hedges of the labyrinth. The phoenix chased after Everett, her magical body tearing loose the magic held trapped all around the palace grounds. Lines of spells whipped through the air, lashing like ropes torn free in a hurricane. Wind, wrapped in broken spells, slashed through the air, slicing through buildings, street lamps, and electric power lines. Chunks of rock, wood and metal fell all around him.

Everett's soul slid by Drake, phoenix in pursuit. Everett doubled back as the phoenix crashed into the South Court bell tower, sending the bell flying with a deafening clang into an adjacent streetlight. Everett's soul came to rest just in front of Drake. Everett's transparent, spectral eyes looked directly into Drake's, pleading to be saved, and for a moment their full history passed between them. Everett's kindness, his betrayal.

Drake shook his head and stepped back as the phoenix brought her mouth down over Everett, devouring him utterly. She reared up, blasted straight into the night sky, toward the Ghost Star and the pulsing rent between the worlds. She disappeared into the fissure and the night grew quiet. Drake could finally hear the sound of distant sirens getting closer and also the muffled sobs of Adam's frightened soulless body.

Drake bent, eased Adam's jaw open and let Adam's soul slide into his open mouth. Adam swallowed easily. A shudder passed through him, then his eyes grew bright and the muscles of his face tightened into an expression. Amazement.

188

"Where is Everett?" Adam sounded loud and dull.

"Gone." Drake mouthed the word. He pointed up at the Ghost Star.

"Then we're safe?"

Drake nodded.

"But everything's still on fire," Adam remarked.

Drake nodded and shrugged. He pointed at the fire truck bursting through the South Court gate.

"We'll be all right then." Adam sagged against Drake. "You know, I have an ear ache."

Drake held him, gently rocking, until the firefighters cleared a path to safety.

Epilogue

Though the king offered to bestow upon Drake the title of royal magician, Drake refused, on the grounds that he preferred to have more free time than the position allowed. Most courtiers greeted this announcement with thinly veiled relief. Drake, with his paladin-like goodness and populist leanings, was not the sort of magician who would be sympathetic to the complicated lives of the inhabitants of the Courts of the Four Directions.

As his reward, in addition to breathtaking quantity of money, Drake negotiated to have the magical ban removed from Thomas Myrdin, so long as the boy changed his name and did not try to contact any of his former associates in the palace. King Louis agreed and Thomas Myrdin became Tom Gantry, the apprentice and heir to the current Guardian of the City.

Lady Langdon referred Adam to a physical magician who was able to partially restore his hearing and manufactured two tiny, golden hearing aids inhabited by the souls of rabbits that helped him to achieve parity with the average city dweller. He took up his guitar again but did not play as loudly as before. Sudden noises now made him jumpy.

He stayed with Drake for a full month while he recovered from the operation and from the experience in general. They spent most of their time in bed. Mostly sleeping.

Mostly.

But eventually Adam's leave of absence came to an end. Drake drove him back to the West Court Palace on a cool September morning. At seven o'clock that same evening, Drake's buzzer rang. He wanted it to be Adam and knew it would not be and knew also that Adam's departure had brought him very close to tears. He let Nancy answer, bending more closely over his calculations, losing himself in math.

A few minutes later he smelled light, woody cologne. Adam stood in his study doorway, dressed in his formal suit, guitar case in hand.

Drake closed his notebook, careful not to speak right away so that his voice would not crack.

"Do you plan to finally finish your recital?"

"How did you know?"

"The large instrument reveals your intentions." Drake pointed down at Adam's guitar case. Adam broke into a smile.

"It sounds so dirty when you say it that way." He set his guitar case down and walked—no, not walked—swaggered into the room.

Drake found himself, to his shame, blushing. How Adam Wexley could disarm him so completely, Drake never understood. Good looks could not account for all of it.

Adam fell onto Drake's sofa, languorously, as if he planned to stay there for the rest of his life. He closed his eyes and sighed. His body was in so complete a repose that Drake felt compelled to draw closer, sit on the edge of the couch, lay his hand on Adam's stomach.

"I realized I'd left something," Adam said.

"Your soul? I was going to give it back to you. I have the contract in my desk."

"Why give it back? If I return to the West Court, they'll just demand I offer it to them again. It's the standard contract for any courtier. Since you already own me, I was hoping to stay here. I've become very partial to this couch."

Drake heard no hint of resentment in Adam's voice, nor did he hear resignation. Adam merely stated the fact of his existence with no drama. Drake found it both gratifying and sad. He allowed himself to lean into Adam's shoulder.

"I don't keep bound servants. I must give you back your soul. But you can stay here for as long as you like."

"That's good," Adam said sleepily, "because Karl's waiting downstairs with my suitcases. I was hoping you'd buzz him up."

Drake smirked and pushed himself up off the now-smug Adam. He said, "Your wish is my command."

About the Author

Nicole Kimberling lives in Bellingham, Washington with her partner, Dawn Kimberling, two bad cats and approximately 100,000 bees. Her novel, Turnskin, won the Lambda Literary Award for Science Fiction, Fantasy & Horror. She is the editor for Blind Eye Books.

In a future ruled by superstition and fear,
wanting the wrong man can be deadly.

Dragon's Kiss
© 2009 Ally Blue
A Mother Earth story.

The rules governing a Pack-Brother's existence are simple. Love your Brothers. Protect each other and your Tribe with your life. Seek sex only within the bonds of Brotherhood, or your life is forfeit. The laws are harsh, but fair. Or so Bear has always thought. Then he and his Brother Lynx capture a stranger in the Carwin Tribe's outlying lands—Dragon, a Brother from a distant Pack, banished from his Tribe for the crime of challenging things he shouldn't.

Dragon intrigues Bear from the start, and not just because of his exotic beauty. Interest in the decadent old world is discouraged in this post-Change society. Dragon is the first person Bear's ever known, other than himself, who's curious about the vanished past. That kinship sparks a forbidden attraction between them. An attraction which is, if they give in to it, punishable by death.

In the space of a day, everything Bear was raised to believe is called into question, and he must make a life-changing decision—follow the law, or follow his heart.

Warning: This book contains ropes, oil, primitive post-apocalyptic cultures and gay sex in the dirt.

Available now in ebook from Samhain Publishing.

Enjoy the following excerpt from Dragon's Kiss...

Bear pulled out more cured meat and tossed it to Lynx. "Who's got first watch?"

"Me. You had last watch before we got started this morning, so you need the rest more." Lynx tore off a hunk of meat with his teeth, chewed, and swallowed. "We'll leave at first light. That way we'll make it home well before dark."

Dragon's gaze flitted between them. In the firelight, his eyes were a pale, almost silvery gray. "I heard Carwin Tribe lives inside Char. That true?"

It didn't surprise Bear that Dragon had heard of the ruined city which surrounded Carwin's walls on all sides. By all accounts, Char was the place where the old civilization had made its last stand after the Change. They'd done their best to keep the old ways alive—evil, wicked ways, according to everything Bear had learned growing up—and keep the Mother's punishment at bay. It hadn't done any good in the end. Less than fifty years after the oceans first began to rise and the human race realized the enormity of its sins against the Earth Mother, Char had fallen into the same chaos that had already destroyed the rest of civilization.

All that remained of Char now was a sprawl of crumbling ruins and a large collection of machines and other artifacts which no one fully understood. Dangerous predators prowled Char's streets, which made traveling between Carwin's walled central city and the outlying tribal lands risky. At least it discouraged the nightfeeders and occasional bands of murderous outcasts from approaching Carwin City.

"Carwin's just inside Char," Bear confirmed. "It was a ruin before the tribe settled there and fixed it up."

Dragon's head tilted sideways. He shot a glance at Lynx, who was poking at the fire, then pinned Bear with a curious look. "So they didn't build it? It was already there?"

This was Bear's favorite story, and he couldn't see any harm in telling it. After all, it wasn't a story of the old world, was it? Tales of Carwin's settlement were allowed. Resting his elbows on his knees, he adopted the tone he half-remembered his mother using when he was a small child, before the tribe's Seer spotted him as Pack and took him from his home.

"When the founders of the Carwin Tribe were traveling through Char looking for a place to settle," he began, "they came to an old road, the kind people used before the Change. On the other side of the road was a huge, wide field, and in the middle of the field was a city inside a wall."

"Carwin." Dragon's eyes were wide, his voice no more than a breath.

Encouraged, Bear nodded. "This city was like nothing they had ever seen. Strange shapes rose up over the walls, like the skeletons of mountains. One shape pointed straight to the sky like a needle. The people were scared, of course, but the walls of the city were tall and thick, and inside were enough buildings to shelter ten times the people they had. And even then, the Carwin Pack was strong enough to defeat any enemy within or without the walls."

Leaning forward, Dragon stared at Bear with a strange fire in his eyes. "What did they find there? They must've found something from the old world. Books, machines, something. What did they find?"

Startled, Bear shook his head. "Buildings. Nightfeeders. Wild dogs, cats, other animals. Those weird metal skeletons, whatever they were. They're still there, actually. They're rusted, parts of them have fallen off, but they're mostly still there.

There used to be little carts on them. Some of the carts are still inside ruined buildings at the base of the skeletons."

"And that's it?"

Bear chewed his bottom lip, torn. He'd seen the things the council and the tribe elders called *photographs*, some of them more than fifteen generations old. The first tribe members had encased them in a tough, transparent, flexible substance to preserve them for all time. The photographs depicted a world beyond imagination. A world where giant metal birds filled the sky and magic boxes could show a person things that were happening so far away it would take weeks to walk there. According to Mother Rose, the Carwin Tribe's founders had discovered the photographs in a pile of books, papers and clothes alongside four huddled corpses inside one of Carwin's many buildings.

The problem was, Bear wasn't supposed to know that. He'd overheard it at a council meeting when he was nine and he, Rabbit and Lynx had snuck into the council room and hidden in the wine cabinet. So he couldn't very well tell Dragon, in spite of the oath he'd taken as a Pack Brother to be truthful. He doubted that oath applied to situations like this anyway.

"No," he said after a long silence. "They didn't find anything else."

With a sigh, Dragon slumped where he sat. He picked crusted leaves off his knee. "I bet they did. Your Mother and your council just don't say so, because they don't want you to know. But they know something about it."

Shocked, Bear stared into the flames. He didn't dare look at Lynx for fear his expression would give him away. He often wished he could go back in time, just for a day, to glimpse a life that had vanished forever when the Earth Mother took back what was Hers.

He knew better than to express that desire. Lynx had never understood Bear's fascination with tales of the world before the change. *A Pack Brother shouldn't walk around with his head in the clouds*, he always said whenever Bear broached the subject. But nothing could stop Bear from dreaming of that lost world sometimes, when the nights were hot and restless.

Glancing at Dragon, Bear saw a faraway look in the man's eyes. A look Bear knew he himself wore when he was daydreaming about the distant past. As if he could feel Bear looking at him, Dragon blinked and met his gaze. Bear smiled. Dragon smiled back, and Bear felt a jolt go through him. He looked away, heart racing. He didn't want to feel this drawn to a man he couldn't have. Especially a man who might be a murderer, or worse.

"I'm gonna get some sleep." Bear stretched out on his back, keeping Dragon's rope looped around his wrist. "Dragon, you might as well get some rest too."

"You want me to take the rope?" Lynx asked, moving to a position where he could see into the darkness outside while still keeping an eye on Dragon.

"No. I'll wake up if he moves." Bear yawned and shut his eyes, trying to ignore Dragon's tantalizing nearness. "Don't forget to wake me up for my watch, Lynx. Just because you *can* stay up a whole day and night doesn't mean it's a good idea."

Lynx laughed. "Shut up and go to sleep, Bear."

Bear smiled. Just before he drifted off to sleep, he felt the rope move as Dragon shifted. His fingers tightened, making sure Dragon stayed close.